Open up The Unseen Blossom wonder, poetry and magnificent i and L'mere Younossi have created a l quest for wisdom and truth. It's a wo.........., ... to the world about all that is good in Afghan culture and all that is good in us. A terrific achievement!

Deborah Ellis is an award-winning author, a feminist and a peace activist. Deborah penned the international bestseller The Breadwinner Trilogy, which has been published around the world in seventeen languages and debuted as a feature animated film. She has achieved international acclaim with more than thirty books to her credit. She has won the Governor General's Literary Award, the Ruth Schwartz Award, the Middle East Book Award, Sweden's Peter Pan Prize, the Jane Addams Children's Book Award and the Vicky Metcalf Award for a Body of Work. She has received the Ontario Library Association's President's Award for Exceptional Achievement, and she has been named to the Order of Canada.

www.deborahellis.com

§

The Unseen Blossom reminds me of the classic One Thousand and One Nights, which as a kid I read about, well, a thousand and one times. Like the classic, this novel has a love story at its heart. Readers would be forgiven for thinking the book was crafted by seasoned writers. While technically written for young adults it reads like a literary novel. Descriptions of the gardens through which our protagonists travel are intricate and written poetically. The writers make some profound visionary statements, including references to the connection between love and the unlocking of human potential, and imploring humanity to protect and nurture the environment on earth and perhaps beyond. This Eastern fairytale is recommended to readers of all ages and cultures.

www.visionaryfictionalliance.com/the-unseen-blossom-a-visionary-fiction-book-review-by-saleena-karim

Saleena Karim is an independent researcher and writer from Nottingham, England. She is also a co-founder of the Visionary Fiction Alliance. Best known for the political biography Secular Jinnah & Pakistan, her novel Systems is inspired by a real visionary idea born in history.

www.visionaryfictionalliance.com/saleena-karim

§

The tale of The Unseen Blossom *starts with the serendipitous friendship formed between co-authors L'mere and Zlaikha, and without their friendship* The Unseen Blossom *may have stayed unseen.* The Unseen Blossom *is a book I truly believe people of any age will be able to resonate with. It is reminiscent of classic tales of adventure like* The Wizard of Oz, Treasure Island, *and Homer's* Odyssey. *Younossi and Samad do a marvelous job at drawing parallels between the reality we live in and the quaint world they've created. The themes explored in* The Unseen Blossom *are that of morality, innocence, love, and the exploration of the desire for peace. Younossi and Samad have created a beautiful and poetic novel that anyone can read effortlessly. It is important to note that a portion of the proceeds* The Unseen Blossom *makes will be donated to help children living in war-torn and impoverished places.*

Reviewed by Justine Reyes for *Readers' Favorite,* **Five Stars**

www.readersfavorite.com

§

The Unseen Blossom is a charming story, a gentle fairy tale that has grown out of the very rocky and violent reality of Afghanistan. This delightful story reminds one of all that remains good and hopeful in the soul of Afghans.

Ambassador Ronald E. Neumann is the author of The Other War: Winning and Losing in Afghanistan, and former United States Ambassador to Afghanistan. He is the current president of the American Academy of Diplomacy in Washington, D.C.

§

The Unseen Blossom *is a novel about love, humanity, and deep interconnection of humans, nature, and past, present, and the future time. The novel is filled with rich poetic language, mystic philosophy, and beauty of universal and culture specific wisdom. The authors' distinct literary talent to show beauty, humanity, love, and hope through a rich poetic and unmatched language is unique, highly sophisticated, and commendable. I most highly recommend this beautiful novel to anyone who is interested in humanity, universal message of love, interconnectedness, and a hopeful future.*

Dr. Nahid Aziz is an Associate Professor at the American School of Professional Psychology. She provides training and conducts research on diversity issues in clinical psychology, including refugees and immigrants' mental health as well as psychosocial issues in conflict and post-conflict countries. Dr. Aziz was the recipient of the Outstanding Dissertation Award which was a clinical manual for mental health professionals working with Afghan refugee women. She is the Vice President of AEBT, a non-profit organization which provides health and education services in Afghanistan. She is also the Co-Chair of the Afghanistan Mental Health Workgroup at SAMHSA.

§

The Unseen Blossom *is a perfect read for everyone all over the world, no matter what age. The book narrates the journey two young protagonists, who are each defined by a strong moral compass, in search for the magical, unseen, and undiscovered beauty offered by nature; a theme that is universal and adaptable for all cultures, times, and people. A highly recommended read.*

Varaidzo Kativhu (Miss Varz) is an undergraduate at Lady Margaret Hall, University of Oxford, England. Miss Varz is an award-winning activist, public speaker, Youtuber, *BBC Presenter, and seen on BBC News, ITV News, The Guardian, The Economist, The Sunday Times,* and other outlets. She campaigns for education and the empowerment of under-represented students.

THE UNSEEN BLOSSOM

a novel by

Zlaikha Y. Samad and L'mere Younossi

The Unseen Blossom

Copyright 2018 ©Zlaikha Y. Samad and L'mere Younossi

Third Edition

All rights reserved. No part of this publication may be reproduced, stored in a retrieval system, or transmitted in any form or by any means, electronic, mechanical, photocopying, recording, or otherwise, without written permission of the authors, except for a brief quotation in a book review.

ISBN 978-0-9981036-5-5 (Print)
ISBN 978-0-9981036-6-2 (eBook)

This is a work of fiction. Names, characters, places, events and incidents are either the products of the authors' imagination or used in a fictitious manner. Any resemblance to actual persons, living or dead, or actual events is purely coincidental.

The Unseen Blossom

Acknowledgements

It is with utmost pleasure and honor that we would like to express our heartfelt gratitude to all who contributed in making our dreams come into existence.

We would like to express our special thanks to everyone who kindly helped in the editing, proofreading, designing, and publishing of all three editions of this book.

Love and respect,

L'mere & Zlaikha

Contents

THE STORY WITHIN THE STORY..................................xv

THE BEGINNING..1

CHAPTER ONE..5
   THE GARDEN OF ALI MARDAN
   THE OUTWARD JOURNEY

CHAPTER TWO..13
   THE FIRST ENCOUNTER

CHAPTER THREE..33
   THE GARDEN OF TULIPS

CHAPTER FOUR...63
   THE GARDEN OF LILY PONDS

CHAPTER FIVE...113
   THE GARDEN OF ROSES

CHAPTER SIX..165
   THE HOMEWARD JOURNEY

CHAPTER SEVEN..191
   THE NEW BEGINNING

RESOURCES..211

ABOUT THE AUTHORS..217

THE STORY WITHIN THE STORY

Two Strangers and a Social Media Glitch

Madeena D. Sadozai

I, a young editor, am pleased to share the story of this book's creation, which took place in the digital realm.

It all began in January of 2016. My mother was active on Facebook and an unusual website glitch drew her attention to a distant familiar acquaintance. Surprisingly, it turned out to be destiny. After a short period of time, they grew to be good friends. I soon realized my mom may have very well found her "soul friend" in L'mere.

It goes without saying that miracles come when you least expect them. Before the social media glitch, my mother purchased a bracelet of a single golden tree, small in size, yet grand in meaning. Three months later, she began writing about a fig tree.

After the immense Virginia snowfall of 2016 passed and before the spring blossomed, L'mere messaged my mother a question that would change both of their lives forever: "Have you ever seen a fig tree blossom?"

L'mere always wished to write a fairytale surrounding the idea of the blossomless fig tree. However, his decision to ask my mom to write the story did not occur until she started to experience surreal feelings surrounding the book. A nagging inner voice urged her to pursue the matter. L'mere, a spiritual soul himself, was moved to ask my mom to write after having similar intuitions. L'mere's dreams, recounted in his biography, sealed the deal. At that, my mother and her co-author began the writing process.

The first six chapters were written before the two ever met. Come August, my family took a trip to New York, where L'mere and my mom met for a few short hours. Interestingly, this book was written with the help of Facebook, phone calls, texts, and the United States Postal Service.

The *Unseen Blossom* was completed on September 7, 2016 at 11:01 AM.

Throughout the years, L'mere had not divulged the secret of his book, despite coming across a multitude of talented individuals. He never sought to become a co-author until the day he became friends with my mother. During the process of writing *The Unseen Blossom*, I watched my mom struggle yet overcome, laugh and cry, research, reflect, ponder, create, and have unbelievable spiritual experiences. Above all, she grew as a new writer.

I, Madee, am a book enthusiast. I have been blessed with the soul of a musician and the mind of a writer. At the present moment, I am sixteen years old, and I recommend buying a few copies to be gifted to members of my generation. That being said, this story has no limits and belongs to everyone, regardless of age or aptitude. Believe me, in sharing this book, you too will have a hand in spreading peace, humor, and love, just as this book intends.

I would like to sincerely thank my mother and L'mere for encouraging and trusting me to assist with editing and contributing to their heartwarming story.

In addition, I would like to thank my dad, Wais Sadozai, for his kind and patient encouragement in supporting us throughout the entire process by offering his astute technical expertise. We thank you!

Moreover, a portion of the proceeds from the sale of this book will be donated to helping war-torn and impoverished children, the most vulnerable and helpless citizens of the world.

The Beginning

No man has ever attained the knowledge to explain the mystery of the fig blossom. No one has ever seen the fig flower. Never has its image touched the iris of sight in day's bright light. Here is a tale as old as time itself, shared hand-to-hand as one would carefully transfer an heirloom. It has been traded and carried across valleys, over the peaks of mountains, through the depths of seas, across never-ending deserts, and onwards throughout the world. Much like this story, the fig tree is old—it bears the most ancient fruit of all, cultivated in Afghanistan for centuries.

It is said of this blossom: "If you doubt this phenomenon, such an extraordinary wonder, then ask yourself: have you ever seen a fig tree bloom?"

The mystery of the fig tree's unseen blossom remained unexplained and never entirely explored to its depths. The wondrous flower holds the beauty of the journey on which you are set to embark. It is one that requires a fresh perspective to unfold the mystery of this heavenly, magical fruit.

History has shown how the fig tree provides for the many who have come across it, beginning with its service to Adam and Eve in the Garden of Eden as a shield of modesty and humility. The presence of the leaves of a fig tree prevented their defiance of all nature and set the course of humanity in perpetuity.

Our story begins in the place of all places, the oldest of all old cities, close to a palace of kings and royals. Hidden from sight, but not too far away, the river emerges and meets the center of city life. It is a place called The Garden of Ali Mardan, perfectly situated in the most archaic of cities, Kabul. Inside the garden is a world of wonder and absolute amazement; it is encircled by walls of trees, plants of all sizes, and colorful flowers. They are both seen and unseen, touched and untouched, by the eyes and hands of mankind. What makes this environment singularly unique is the very existence of a massive, long-standing fig tree in the middle of a circular stone enclosure.

It was a day in *bahaar* (spring) unlike any other, and the breeze of life lovingly played with the buds of a new beginning.

Chapter 1

The Garden of Ali Mardan
The Outward Journey

Fifty days ago, she counted fifty figs. She set them side-by-side and arranged them in three neat rows inside a clear glass jar with an air-tight cover. She closed her eyes, vowing to feast on one fig a day. She always did this when she was getting ready to make a wish. She knew that, by making a wish, she was putting her spiritual energy out into the vast, unknown universe to travel near, far, around and around. Her wishes always found their way back to her, and, eventually, each one came true.

Today, she ate the last fig; her heart grew fuller now more than it had during each passing day, and she was utterly amused as her wishes found their way back to it.

With a book and pen in hand, she walked towards the same familiar path, a narrow sidewalk worn from her footprints of comings and goings. She headed north towards the Kabul River, leading to the bridge that she routinely crossed. Customarily, she would stop to admire the clarity of the water running through the city, purifying the troubled lives of the bustling passersby. She resumed her north-bound walk to cross the tiny *Pul-e-Larzanak* (shaky bridge), and kept onwards until she reached her favorite spot.

Yes, it was her very own hideaway, encircled by an array of flowers that beamed at her with all of nature's colors and scents. Lush green leaves enveloped the cushiony ground where she stood. Here, to the left of The Garden of Ali Mardan's main entrance, she was entirely hidden from view.

It was in this garden that her imagination was most inspired. She felt as though this was a sacred place, and here she would hide with her inner most reflections and the never-ending dreamlike images that filled her senses. Indeed, her home away from the chaos of real life was right under that tree. The tree grew as she did, from a child to a young lady. Growing alongside her, the tree soon felt larger than life itself.

Standing under the tree, she looked up with a radiant smile. She greeted the tree as she always did, by admiring its green leaves and sharp brown branches with plentiful offerings. The tree asked for nothing in return but reverence for its prominent and magnificent stature.

She recalled sitting with her back to the garden as a young child, facing the familiar tree trunk. Often, she would hug its rough, weathered surface, always feeling as though it returned her hug and offered inner peace. Over the years, she spoke to the tree, letting her words echo stories from her fertile imagination. The words whispered from her lips leisurely journeyed up and down the tree branches, touching each and every piece of foliage, their surfaces greener than the greenest jadeite.

The words she uttered today from her heart were

the same words as those from yesterday and those from the past months and years: her undeniable wish for love to sprout in the hearts of all humanity, like wildflowers endlessly growing in the fields.

She recalled the tale of a certain ancient flower. Many curious men of all statures left their homes and families to seek the bloom of the fig tree. Alas, they were never to return, forever vanishing to distant lands. However, if one could indeed find that most precious and rare fig blossom, it was said that entire nations could attain everlasting love, peace, and harmony.

Today, her thoughts wandered off to faraway lands that she had never seen before. An odd notion came to her – perhaps it was not a *man* who was to find this unseen flower of love. Perchance, it was a quest for a resilient and brave woman. Yes! Though she adored flowers, she was not delicate. She often ventured into the neighborhoods in disguise, and recognized how strong and courageous she was compared to the boys she saw there.

She remembered witnessing a fight between several boys on one of the backroads of Kabul. She was usually able to stop these fights by condemning their lapse in morality with firm authority. That time, however, with her animated hand gestures, she accidentally knocked her hat off and it fell to the ground, revealing her long black hair. She could still see them gawking at her, wide-eyed in bewilderment. Their faces remained etched in her mind, caught off guard by her defiant presence. The boys gasped, mouths agape in shock, and took off running in the opposite direction as though they had never seen a girl before.

While sitting in the accompaniment of her soul's reflections, she felt the heat rise around the garden and wished she had some ice-cold water to drink. Indeed, it was warmer than the usual temperature for this time of the year. It made her feel not only thirsty, but also lazy and a bit woozy. Just for a moment, she decided to lean back on the trunk of the tree to allow its leafy branches to cool her off in their shade.

She relaxed under the tree. Surely, the heat must have tired her after she spent a few moments gathering flowers, a small bouquet of all colors and shapes. Flowers fed her senses with their soft scents, delicate yet perfectly arranged petals, stems of various lengths, and rich green leaves. Frankly, she could live happily ever after in fields of all types of flora.

Once a week, she made sure to take a bouquet of flowers home to be placed in a round ceramic vase. Its edges of red and golden trimmings always caught the splendid sunrays at both sunrise and sunset. She deliberately chose that particular spot for the flower vase: in the corner of her room, close to the mirror. From time to time, she would catch her own reflection in this relic of a mirror, passed down to her from her grandmother. To her astonishment, the flood of sun rays brightened her room with shades of yellow and orange, indistinguishable from the beams that lit the garden where her tree was proudly grounded.

The cooling, twirling summer breeze brought her thoughts back to the garden. She reminded herself not to get back home too late because her mother was very strict and did not allow her to miss supper at eight. Nonetheless, what harm could a moment of relaxation cause?

It was at that precise moment when she heard a loud and disturbing crack from the other side of the tree trunk.

Chapter 2

The First Encounter

She sprang to her feet in such a fast and reckless manner that the grass swayed under her. Startled by the sudden disruption, she looked around with piercing eyes, scouring the garden's corners for intruders. Never before had she heard such an unsettling, sharp sound, nor had she ever seen a silhouette so transient that it disappeared in the blink of an eye. How very odd! But where did it go?

She was uncertain if she had seen the shadow of a man or an animal. Perhaps it could have been a ghost. She remembered hearing tales about this very garden, tales that told of how the fig tree was protected by all sorts of celestial beings, fairies, and even dour spirits. She knew they meant no harm; they were solely there as guardians, protecting the grounds and the splendor of the tree in the heart of the garden.

More questions sprinted through her mind as she heard the same crackling sound over and over again, leaving her a bit unnerved. She was surprised as a spark of tenacity ignited her courage to fend off any malevolent presence. Her thoughts implored her to be cautious as she checked where the shadow had disappeared. Vigilantly, she moved towards the other side of the tree trunk where, without a flicker of a doubt, the shadow had vanished.

There were no visible signs of a disturbance – the tree looked the same as it had before. She examined the tree trunk; her eyes moved up and down in a meticulous search for any details she may have missed. Her eyes widened as she spotted a gap in the tree's trunk. She had examined every inch of her tree all of her life, but she had never seen this gash before. She moved closer, until her nose was practically touching the trunk. She peered at the gap until she had squished her whole face against the tree.

A ray of light shone through the small slash. She squinted harder, bringing her left hand up and apprehensively touching the ever so tiny gap.

From inside the tree trunk, she was abruptly pulled in by what seemed like the strong grip of an actual human hand. It held on tight, squeezing all of her fingers as if to break her bones. She was suddenly faint and breathless, gasping as she felt her entire body lift into the air for what seemed like only a second or two. Like a small pebble ricocheting off the surface of a calm pond, she was flung onto the ground with such ferocity that it made her bounce right off. She knew that she was no longer in the Garden of Ali Mardan.

After a few long seconds, she managed to recover from the abrupt shock and come back to her senses. It was then she realized that the shadow she had seen now stood over her. She looked up and saw a tall young man peering down at her with fascination.

They stared at each other with panicked eyes and intense, puzzled expressions. It felt as though endless minutes passed. She suddenly snapped out of her trance and furiously jumped to her feet. She took a few steps back from him, yelling her thoughts as they came to her.

"Who are you? Where am I? Was it you who pulled me through the tree trunk?"

Her questions grew angrier. "How is that even possible? How dare you throw me on the ground in such a vicious way! And why are you staring at me with such an intense glare? Do not even try coming close. I am capable of hurting you and giving you a bloody nose. I have done it before to boys just like you with that same repugnant look on their faces. I will hurt you if you try to get closer! I've warned you!"

She felt her familiar resilience and strength return, coursing through the muscles in her arms and legs. Ready in attack mode, she took her first real look at her mysterious captor. He was a tall brute, resembling a wild and ferocious man, with way too much curly hair in unruly long waves that gradually crept down to the nape of his neck.

Her arms were bent to throw a punch and her feet were planted strongly on the ground, ready to jump in the air and throw kicks as high as the young man's head. Her eyes never blinked nor broke their intense stare. She was ready for whatever was coming her way. She took a slow, shaky breath.

Unpredictably, the stranger's eyes softened. His face broke into a brilliant smile. The muscles in his neck relaxed, his shoulders dropped with ease, and his stance became less threatening.

"Dear Princess Zuli, please accept my heartfelt apologies for the fright I may have caused you, but I assure you that I had no choice. It was a duty I had to fulfill without any further delay."

Zuli was stunned into silence.

He continued, "Forgive me yet again. Where are my manners? Allow me to introduce myself. My name is Lamar."

Not knowing what else to do amid her silence, Lamar continued to speak.

"We have been brought together today because of my grandfather. He was an accomplished nobleman who was highly respected for his deep spiritual connections to other realms beyond ours. And my father possessed all the same qualities. Sadly, he and my mother died last year, leaving me alone in the midst of all this war and chaos."

She cut him off rather rudely to say, "Never refer to me as princess, it is an utmost frivolous title. How do you know my name? I don't know you at all. I have never seen nor met you until just minutes ago. I would've remembered you if I had met you; I have an excellent memory. Have you been following me? How very rude! I'm warning you to keep your distance."

Upon hearing her statements and admiring the irate look on her face, Lamar could not do anything but smile even more brilliantly at her. The smile seemed to irritate Zuli even more, but he responded anyway.

"To answer one of your questions: yes, indeed, I have been following you for an entire lifetime and have been waiting for you for what seems like an eternity."

As the words left his lips and the wind swiftly blew them towards her, she felt her heartbeat skip a beat. Odd, unfamiliar feelings gripped her heart.

She looked directly at him and said, "I don't understand anything that you're saying. Again, I have never set eyes on you before." Zuli folded her arms in front of her chest.

"This place is my hideaway! For years I have come here, and I have never seen you, or anyone else for that matter. You must be mad; that's all I can conclude!"

Lamar continued as if he had not heard the words she hurled at him.

"I fully understand your concerns and apprehension. However, if you would allow me, I can explain the entire story in no time."

She did not respond, which gave him a chance to clarify. After all, she was highly intrigued by the fanciful events that had unfolded within minutes, turning an ordinary day into a dream-like fairytale.

"You see, growing up, I was very close to my grandfather and spent my entire childhood with him. My grandfather was a simple and dignified gentleman possessing all elements of humanity. He was a true believer in fairness for mankind. However, he was famous for having keen insights and innate magical intuitions about the stories that had been passed down for generations."

Zuli listened with great intent as Lamar continued. "These stories had forever been regarded as entirely mythical, but my grandfather possessed an awareness of the magical realm. He was the Keeper of the Magical Fig Tree, the same tree you have visited since childhood.

"I remember one day in the springtime as I walked to the local fruit shop, I saw that all of the trees lining the street were in full bloom and would soon produce delicious fruits. However, for the first time, I noticed that the fig tree had no blossom, yet had already produced small figs. I walked down the narrow path by the town square, and it seemed this strange occurrence continued behind me. I headed straight to that very garden, the Garden of Ali Mardan, to investigate the large fig tree and understand what I had discovered before discussing it with my grandfather."

"Zuli," Lamar said, "Only I hold the key to the fig tree. My grandfather left it to me. He told me about it before his death. As I've said, he was a man of spiritual depths. He knew precisely at what hour of which day he would pass from this realm into the next. He asked me to sit with him, and it was on the day of his passing that he shared the true story of the fig tree that stands eternally in the Garden of Ali Mardan.

"He told me that I must be patient and wait until I was of age in order to be able to gain access to the magical tree. Exactly three years and three days after his death, a wooden box was delivered to me in the *mouchy* shop (shoe repair shop). It was placed on the floor by the right side of my bed at precisely one minute after midnight, the moment I turned eighteen. I recalled my grandfather telling me that I could only use its contents after turning eighteen. Just before taking his last breath, my grandfather recited the following verses to me, to steer me in the right direction at the commencement of my journey: *Here I am, a heart of dust. Go seek the unseen fig blossom. Know that only with the hidden eye of my core existence, and from the garden of my heart, can I hope to make it visible to the eyes of the seekers. I shall be a guiding light in all places on the path of your journey forward.*"

He continued, "I, Lamar, am now the keeper of the magical key and you, Zuli, are the chosen one. As you know, seven days ago you turned eighteen years old. This is why you were able to cross over to this side and join me on the quest to find the legendary fig blossom.

"I understand you have wished upon the fig tree over a thousand times, if not more, and your mind has been set on making this journey alone. Please know our fates were designed otherwise. You must realize that two people are needed for this endeavor; otherwise, the mystical forces will not allow us to go one step beyond the grand rock resting behind you."

Zuli turned around. Sure enough, behind her sat a colossal rock. It was so large that it resembled a miniature mountain. *How on earth did I not see such an enormous rock?* She turned back around to face Lamar, who was still talking.

"My grandfather told me that two people must join hands, hearts, and minds to embark on this quest. He firmly believed that anything could be achieved if people joined forces equally and devotedly. Inside the wooden box by my bed that night was a magical branch, meticulously wrapped in many folds of colorful lace –"

"A tree branch was wrapped in layers of lace? How

odd! I dare you to show me, if you are telling me the truth," demanded Zuli.

He responded calmly, "I shall show you the magical tree branch. But before I do, you must listen to what I have to say."

Zuli nodded.

"Carefully keep my words in your memory, to remind you during foggy moments on this journey. The never-seen fig blossom was a gift from another domain. Our fate brought us together for the magical fig tree to reveal the splendor of its heart and soul to you, Zuli, daughter of the king who rules our nation. Through the inherent voice of wisdom and the purity of our souls, we must find the fig blossom to remove the curtain of mystery from this legendary story. With the help of strong hearts and resilient minds, it shall be possible to find the mystical flower. Only then will we be able to present it to our beloved nation. The charmed fig blossom will help heal the sorrow and grief in the hearts of one and all."

Zuli's thoughts wandered from his words to the unsettling issues of the country she loved dearly. It was the single reason she wished upon the figs she consumed daily. As the king's only child, she felt obligated to find the fig blossom. She wished to bring it back to her father. Even he, with all his might and thousands of men, could not bring everlasting peace to his beloved country, Afghanistan. She knew very well that the magical powers of the fig blossom would inevitably ignite wild flames of love and sow the seeds of peace into the blood-drenched soil of the magnificent land.

Zuli always wished to be free of the palace and all its restrictions and she was certainly weary of constantly sneaking out of the palace in disguise. She knew that, if she was caught fleeing, her strict mother, the queen, would sentence her to house arrest until she was either married off or turned 101 years of age.

Besides, she always felt more at ease on the streets of Kabul than within the lush, rich walls of the majestic royal palace. She was, without a doubt, on board with the idea of adventuring. She had always been known to have the spirit of an adventurer, if only given the opportunity.

She recalled one of her quests, a daring undertaking that required much planning and sneaking around, always with the help of her most beloved *aapa* (nanny) Gulnar, her only confidante. On a bright sunny day, she snuck out of the castle with her bike on a quest towards the *Darul Aman* Palace. She was very well aware that girls were not given the same equal privileges and civil liberties as boys. Girls were mostly kept away from the outside world and hidden indoors. This was done to protect their poise and dignity, and to avoid society's harsh judgements and dangers.

She hated such inequality between the two genders with a passion. The day she would be crowned queen of the nation, she would enforce a commonly ignored law already etched in the land's Constitution: freedom for all, regardless of gender, race, ethnicity, status, or religion. Hence, she often left the palace in full disguise so no one would distinguish her from any other man as they passed her on the busy streets of Kabul.

The times she rode her bike outside the palace walls

were the most freeing for Zuli. Often, she roamed without purpose or direction on her bike, moving from street to street, corner to corner, passing fruit shops, mosques, *naan waa'ee* (bread bakeries), *kolcha-froshi* (pastry shops), and *kabobee* (kabob shops). Specifically, she enjoyed observing the countless street vendors perfectly lined up next to one another with their extra-large platters, piled with all sorts of appetizing dried or ripe fruits, candies, and more. Each vendor would shout out their price of the day in hopes of enticing bypassers to make a purchase. Even more so, she loved watching the *kachaloo wa shornakhod waalaa* (potato and chickpea seller).

He peeled the potatoes perfectly and then proceeded to slice them as thin as the sheerest silk. He put a handful of potatoes in an iron bowl and topped them with a full tablespoon of chickpeas. He then poured a generous amount of vinaigrette dressing on them and added red peppers to make it very spicy. She watched people stand there as they consumed the delicious *kachaloo wa shornakhod*. She knew it was customary for everyone to drink up all the dressing from the side of the bowl in order to not waste a drop. The seller would quickly wash the bowl and spoon in a bucket full of water after the customers were long gone.

Zuli recalled the day she ventured from *Shahre-Naw* (new city) towards *Darul Aman* Palace. She passed *Karta-e-Chahar* (the 4th district). Soon after, she passed *Karta-e-Say* (the 3rd district). She biked all the way to a castle she had heard of, but never set eyes upon. She had read in history books that the palace was built in the early 1920s as part of King Amanullah

Khan's efforts to modernize Afghanistan. The palace was a majestic building, modeled after the classic Roman architecture, on a hilltop in the western part of the capital city. For hours, away from her own private castle, she roamed around the grandiose palace.

Sadly, this majestic structure, a nation's proud heritage, lacked proper maintenance and was left in shambles from various civil wars. Zuli biked from one room to the next with ease, making sure she missed no corners as she moved from the inside out. After sometime, she decided to head back home. With Gulnar's help, she was never caught by anyone, even when she got back so very late, just minutes before eight, when dinner was punctually served.

Zuli thought this was, perhaps, her only golden opportunity to venture off with absolute freedom.

Her attention snapped back to Lamar. She realized that he had been speaking the whole time her mind was elsewhere. He now looked at her with a puzzled frown on his face, asking whether she had listened to a word he had said.

She replied rather mockingly, "Yes, of course I listened. What else would I be doing?!"

He ignored her snide remarks. "Now is the time to show you the magical branch. You must come close; I assure you, I will not hurt you. You don't need to fear me."

"I assure *you* that I neither fear you nor am I threatened by you," she snarled.

Zuli took a few steps forward but made certain to leave a generous amount of space between them.

Lamar then took a few more steps towards her, bringing them much closer than she desired. He towered over her with his strong and tall physique. She glanced up at him and realized that he did not look like a monster, after all.

Rather, he looked like an old painting she saw in a book long ago. His deep warm eyes were of the most unusual color. They appeared to be a mix of misty gray and dark caramel, framed with thick lashes. Above his eyes were bushy yet perfectly manicured eyebrows. His nose was straighter than an arrow, and his lips as ample and grand as the words he so constantly spoke. She rounded off her observation by noting his jawline, the strongest she had ever seen and, of course, that brilliant smile Lamar kept flashing at her.

She hastily looked down at his hands, which held a long package enveloped by delicate lace and covered with heaps of rainbow-colored flowers. The wrappings were simply glorious. Carefully, he began to unwrap the laces, layer after layer after layer. Each exposed lace was drenched in radiant colors that Zuli had never before seen, with flowers far more exotic than those she picked for her room from the Garden of Ali Mardan. Zuli watched with what seemed like ceaseless anticipation as she waited for Lamar to finish his tedious unwrapping. Finally, he held up a stick.

Her eyes travelled back up to the face of the young man standing in front of her.

He then explained, "This is the magical branch from the fig tree upon which you have always wished. This branch possesses three wishes. I was told to use the wishes sensibly and cautiously, specifically for this journey."

He extended the branch to her, and Zuli reached for it with both hands in a slow and steady manner. When it contacted her flesh, she sensed a rush, like a surge of light erupting within her soul, running through the chambers of her heart, up her spine, and around and around her being until she felt as bright as the burning sun at high noon. Now, she felt as though she could fly into the sky or pick up the gigantic rock sitting behind her with just one hand.

She noticed that the tree branch was unbendable and sturdy, with gold-coated details along its sides. It was covered in designs and shapes that looked like stars with a half crescent moon, birds, flowers, fish, and much more. The design was finished with what seemed like a handcrafted, exquisite silver tip, which resembled one of the writing instruments her father brought back from one of his journeys.

While holding the magical tree branch in both hands, Zuli felt more powerful than she ever had before. It all came together, solidifying her wishes and aspirations. Now, at this very second, standing in an unfamiliar place with a young man she knew not, she felt a surge of confidence with crystal clarity beyond the shadows of her doubt about the journey ahead. Her daily wish upon the figs gradually began to come true.

As she continued to further examine the magical tree branch, Lamar observed her every move, action, and reaction. He knew exactly the kind of sensations that went through her because he, too, felt the same surge of empowerment within his soul and heart immediately upon holding the magical tree branch in his own bare hands. Even after so many years of watching her comings and goings in the Garden of Ali Mardan, he had never gotten the chance to observe her sharp features from such a close position. He knew that she was as tough as him. He had witnessed her outsmart a few hooligans who had tried to pester her. Yet, he had never noticed her classical beauty.

He found her striking, with her dark velvet brown eyes topped with exquisitely arched eyebrows. Her nose looked regal, a nose fit for a princess. Her face was neither round nor square – in Lamar's opinion, it was perfect. Her lips were full, and had a flawless shape. Zuli's hair was as thick and as black as night itself, with a bounce of curls falling just under her shoulders. She was not very tall but carried herself with pride and poise.

Despite her obvious outer beauty, the purity and kindheartedness of her soul was known to him and him alone. She was a cut-off piece of his own being, his soul, leaving a void within him. At last, unbeknownst to her, their meeting and reunion today filled that empty void.

According to his grandfather, they were old friends from another realm, chosen to take this journey together as one. She knew no details of their history, and he dared not reveal it to her yet. He looked down at her silky black shoes and compared them to his worn out plastic brown ones. She was ordained to rise as the queen of the land; he was destined to be the best shoe repairman. He would forevermore keep his feelings concealed and hidden in the innermost parts of his core. Now, his focus would be entirely on the journey, ensuring the retrieval of the fig blossom. He knew all too well that, upon their return, she would go back to the palace while he would go back to his shop, as predestined by fate.

Zuli realized that she had been examining the branch for the longest time. She looked up at him, now standing very close to her. With hesitation, she took a step back, and asked, "What must we do now?"

Her voice brought him back to the present moment and he responded, "According to my grandfather's instructions, we must each inscribe our names onto the rock behind you. This will ensure our re-entry into the Garden of Ali Mardan.

"Ladies should always go first," Lamar said. "So go ahead and inscribe your name in any style you wish."

They walked towards the massive rock. She took the tree branch in her left hand as if preparing to write on a piece of paper. Nervous, she bent close and began to engrave her name on the surface of the solid rock: Zuli. She handed the branch to Lamar. As he took it from her, he too moved closer to the rock, bent down, and with composure, engraved his name under hers: Lamar.

In an instant, after the silver tip of the tree branch etched the final letter of his name and as he lifted it from the rock's smooth surface, the ground began to rumble beneath their feet. They looked at one another, startled, and took a step backwards. The rock grew to be even more massive than before, resembling a volcano. Through the thick dust flying around them, they could still make out their names on the surface of the rock.

There was a deep gravelly sound, but Lamar's attention was broken by the shrill sound of Zuli's shriek. He turned to see her sprinting away from the protruding boulder, only to trip on the most diminutive pebble and fall face first in the dust.

Lamar wondered what could have stirred such a fearful reaction in Zuli. It was in that moment that he looked back at the rock's grainy surface to see a pair of lips as thin as a slit cut by a very sharp pair of scissors, and two tiny eyes. The rock was alive and staring at them both, whispering their names to himself over and over, almost as if refreshing its memory.

It was then that the rock said, "Come closer; it seems that I have caused a bit of a dust storm and it has obscured my vision."

Apprehensively, they moved closer to the rock and stared into its observant eyes. It spoke with such ease that it left them feeling safer.

"It is so good to see you both. You must not remember me, but I have been with you through many passages of time. I am Adir, your guide, but I am grounded where I am."

He continued, "I am not a rock, but rather an extension of all the mountains encompassing the land you are devoted to."

As he spoke, remnants of some dust came out of his mouth as though he was blowing smoke into the air.

"You have been chosen to embark on this journey together to retrieve the unseen fig blossom. I'm supposed to tell you to take your first steps," Adir said. "You should know that each step is designed not only to guide you, but also to heighten your level of awareness, test your judgements, probe your minds, enlighten your hearts, and help evolve your souls.

Adir looked from Zuli to Lamar. "Remember these teachings well. What you acquire will be the solid foundation for a better future, just as permanent and solid as I. Only through acquiring these lessons will you find the true fig blossom and its wisdom.

"From this point on, go east and only east, towards the direction of the rising sun, until you reach the Garden of Tulips. Though, be warned. There will be countless hindrances to your mission. Not all is how it seems. When your journey ends, go west and only west, where we shall meet again."

Zuli was puzzled. "How will we know when the quest is complete? Will we know where to find you?"

To this, Adir replied, "Oh sweet girl, you will know it deep within your heart." The last words he articulated were, "Safe travels."

32

Chapter 3

The Garden of Tulips

> "One's stagnant being will be forever encapsulated by the past unless the crucial prospect of change is exercised."
>
> ~ *Madeena D. Sadozai*

They embarked on their grand and mystical journey on the eastern pathway. Much like the musings of the Tang dynasty poet, the pair was "gazing to the south, from the eastern peak, the moon appears through the raindrops."

After some time, Zuli felt Lamar's tension; he was quiet and pensive. She, too, felt uneasy because of their seemingly endless wanderings. Still, they practically marched in complete unison. Neither one of them had any idea how far they would have to go before reaching the Garden of Tulips. They were total strangers, yet they were chosen and brought together by fate to search for the mysterious fig blossom.

Although she was anxious, and her mind was preoccupied, Zuli's eyes moved rapidly to take everything in, leaving no site unobserved. This place was like a reverie. She had heard exaggerated fairytales at bedtime, when her grandmother sat by her bed and told her the most mesmerizing stories – tales of gardens filled with rainbows of all colors, and not just any ordinary colors, but even colors unknown to man. Now she was here, amidst ethereal gardens, overwhelmed by the ultimate splendor that she witnessed. She saw no obvious gate out of the garden, yet they continued to march on as they were told by Adir.

They started off strong and fast, moving towards the glowing and looming sun. As the sun bowed down ever so regally from sight, exhaustion came over Lamar. Their pace had slowed and the sky had grown darker. He watched the sun spread a golden glow upon the landscape. The beauty astounded him beyond anything he had imagined, and he knew that he had an imagination like no other. He was reminded of one of his favorite poems by the great poet Hafiz: *Even after all this time the sun never says to the earth, "You owe me." Look what happens with a love like that, it lights the whole sky.* He loved how eloquently Hafiz hinted at giving with abundance and selflessness for the well-being of others.

His mind traveled back in time. As a nineteen-year-old, Lamar had witnessed wars upon wars. There were conflicts between ethnic groups, minorities, and heads of governments in the land he loved. This was the land where his father was born, and it was the same land that received his father buried in its folds. Lamar recalled when he took those few daunting steps toward the huge opening in the earth. Without hesitation, he clutched the old shovel with a strong grip, threw piles and piles of dry soil upon his father's resting body, and watched as he became one with the dust. He refused to let anyone else partake in this task. To Lamar, dust was just dust – until his beloved was placed within it. Then, it became sacred ground. It was no wonder his father admired and regularly quoted the popular Afghan poet, Rabia Balkhi: *Mud smells of roses, as though kneaded with rose water*. He shoveled and shoveled heaps of dry soil over his father's wooden coffin that hot and blessed Friday afternoon. His tears flowed with such ease and urgency that the dry soil was soon drenched. He recollected how much his father had loved the flow of water in rivers, cascading down mountain tops or gushing out of a *cheshma-e-aab* (water spring).

He hoped that his father, a proud man of honor, yet humble to the core, could not see his son's crushing sadness and the tears that now overflowed onto the ground of the land he loved. Even more so, Lamar hoped that, in the short time they spent together, his character had made an everlasting impression on his father.

Lamar had grown into a young man with great eagerness to understand himself and his life in relation to his environment. He was fortunate to be from a well-educated family with a desire for learning. From very early in his childhood, his father had a tremendous impact on Lamar's perception of life within its boundaries.

However, Lamar's sole intention was to find his meaningful purpose in life through his *own* mind's eye. He knew this keenness was instilled in him by both his father and grandfather. His poetic and philosophical nature had its way of pushing and pulling him in different directions at different stages of life. It gradually shaped his ideas of life's meaning, sparking an immense curiosity.

He wanted to understand the corrupt inequalities of his environment. Now and again, he had trouble making sense of it all. It was during these times that he became a deep thinker compared to the other kids around him. They sometimes found him to be too intimidating, or a know-it-all, both of which he thoroughly enjoyed. From a very young age, Lamar thought it imperative to ponder the meanings of various issues independently, rather than be guided step-by-step.

His ultimate wish was for his father to still be alive, and know that Lamar was, indeed, as brave and patriotic as all the men in his family. Much like his grandfather, Lamar believed he had been gifted with an innate conviction about matters of right and wrong.

As they walked, Lamar's thoughts traveled from one memory to the next. He remembered that soon after he buried his father, the war took his extended family, not only by death, but also by ripping generational roots that connected the old and young. Tragically, war wiped out entire identities. War and conflict took what was familiar and, in return, handed back unfamiliar twists designed to wreak havoc on one's measure of tolerance and endurance. Under such hardships, the oppressed either soared above the charring flames of destruction, or were swept away like ashes blown far and wide from the good and familiar. Family, neighbors, and schoolmates were forced to forever carry their memories from their part of the world to one unfamiliar domain after another.

In Lamar's case, despite his grand family and affluent past, the only job he found was at a shoe repair shop. He was turned down from all the other jobs for which he was qualified, even though he was well-educated. What Lamar now lacked was the proper family backing and influence to help secure a decent job. He knew the byproduct of prolonged war was that nobility fell to poverty, and poverty had become a pandemic disease. Regardless, his true identity remained intact and he was proud to earn an income because it allowed him to save his money for a brighter future. Most of his extended family left their homeland to save their own lives as well as their children's.

Like the mesmerizing sun overhead, he decided to stay. He was always drawn to the sun. His dear mother named him Lamar because it means "sun" in Pashto, one of the two official languages spoken in his country, Afghanistan.

People should learn from the humility of the sun, he thought to himself. *The sun, with all its forceful might, dispenses its wholesome glory upon one and all. Its only resolve is warm-heartedness, providing for the continuation of our existence.*

After this simple reflection, Lamar's train of thought was brought to a sudden halt and his mind was silenced by a remarkable sight ahead. He quickly turned to Zuli to point it out, but realized that she had already seen it herself. She stood immobile, her face gleaming and her mouth wide open in disbelief.

In the distance, not too far ahead, there were countless soaring trees of different colors. These were no ordinary trees. They were of every color *except* green, perfectly aligned, making the paths between them look like vibrant tunnels of color. There were rows of purple trees, orange trees, blue trees, yellow trees, and colors never before seen. For each colorful shade, the leaves, the tree trunks, and the ground beneath were the same hue. The birds, insects, and butterflies flying around the trees were the same color. At that instant, they both knew that they had to travel through the tunnels of color in order to reach the Garden of Tulips.

By the time they reached the rows of the first purple trees, the day had fully turned to night. They were tired and in need of much rest. They each picked a tree to lean against for the night so they could catch a few hours of sleep. The purple ground felt like a soft, cushiony bed. The tree felt welcoming when Lamar leaned against it. It molded to his shape and gave him ample support. He noticed that the leaves, which had fallen off the trees in all different sizes and shapes, felt like velvet to the touch.

Lamar watched Zuli find her own comfortable spot further away from him. She sat herself down as a princess would and gathered some leaves. She felt each leaf with her long and lean fingers. She even brought each one close to her nose and smelled it, gently rubbing it against the side of her face. She gathered even more leaves and made a small pile on her lap. From where he was sitting, she looked like a painting amidst the purple. All that was missing was a golden frame to capture the beauty and frame it forever.

She took out her little notebook and began to draw the shapes of the leaves, and wrote word after word, holding the pen in her usual left-handed position.

What a splendid sight in such a heavenly place, Lamar thought to himself, feeling exhaustion take over.

Suddenly, something or someone shook him and, although there was no one there, Lamar jolted out of his deep sleep. He looked around and was instantly filled with serenity and joviality from the overwhelming resonance of birdsong. They sounded like a thousand children singing an upbeat tune of praise. The entire garden was bursting with music.

Even as a child, Lamar had enjoyed music. Later in life, as the proud owner of a small battery-operated radio, he had a chance to listen to classical music. He became a fan of the world's greatest humanitarian and composer, Ludwig von Beethoven. Lamar could not get enough of Beethoven's music, especially his Ninth Symphony. Listening to it triggered a sense of internal longing to expunge years of pain and find solace within. He wondered if Zuli could hear this amazing outdoor symphony of the birds.

Lamar looked across the way and saw Zuli sound asleep. In the early morning light, she was covered in purple leaves, as if a quilt had been sewn together and carefully thrown over her to keep her warm overnight. She must have sensed him gawking at her because she, too, jolted out of her sleep to find him gazing at her with a bemused expression. A hint of a smile crossed her lips as she heard the musical tunes. She gazed back at Lamar in stunned disbelief, which was yet spellbinding to all of his senses.

Their journey through the remaining tunnels of color came to an abrupt end as the ground became the grayest of grays and the air overhead grew gloomy. There was no more looming sun and no more birds; it was chillingly quiet.

Zuli and Lamar cautiously walked on, not knowing which way was east. In the blink of an eye, they were no longer on solid ground. They gave each other one final look of confusion before the sandy earth crumbled under their unsteady feet.

They fell straight down, hitting an earthy surface. There was no time to even breathe a sigh of relief, however, because they again fell through a pitch-black tunnel onto a hair-raising slide. They sped up and down, left and right, in different directions at all speeds. Zuli could do nothing but throw her hands in the air and pray that this was not the end of their short mission.

During the free-fall, Zuli realized that she had lost sight of Lamar. As she thought this, however, she heard a spine-chilling roar behind her, and it was safe to assume that he was, in fact, present. The endless passageway took a sharp turn and Zuli thought she would be thrown face first into the solid wall before her.

After what felt like hours, she began to decrease in velocity. The incline leveled to a flat plane and Zuli came to a halt at the edge of the highest cliff she had ever seen. Before her was a perfectly vertical drop. She propped herself up on her arms, wondering what to do next. She realized she had lost Lamar again. As she began to stand up, however, Zuli felt a forceful shove against her back, knocking the wind right out of her.

She screamed "NOOOO," but it was too late; they both hurtled through the air, pulled down by gravity. In the midst of the fall, Zuli found Lamar's hand. She squeezed it, thinking of the best and worst outcomes, and possibly breaking a bone or two. Thankfully, there was no cluster of jagged, uneven rocks below. Instead, they approached an expansion of color at a mind-boggling speed. Zuli closed her eyes, let go of Lamar's hand, and threw both hands over her face, only to be greeted by the strongest, most delectable fragrance she had ever inhaled. She landed on a bed of tulips and, sure enough, Lamar landed right on her, expelling her very last breath.

Lamar heard Zuli screeching, "Ouch! Get off of me! I believe you broke my back! Get off of me now!"

He was trying his best, but could not find his balance and, before he knew it, she twisted under him, brought her knee up, and kicked him right in the stomach. She then braced both of her hands on his shoulders and pushed him off. Lamar went flying and landed on a patch of tulips. His weight crushed the tulips, which instantly filled the air with aromas as sweet as any flower he had ever smelled. The glorious scents awakened and tickled his olfactory senses. He propped himself up, stood, and observed the fields of tulips. He looked to Zuli, who was still lying in the midst of the flowers. She held a bunch of them in her hand, all squished with broken stems from the fall. Her eyes were closed and she took deep breaths. Lamar was sure that, at any given moment, she would pass out.

Still in pain from being kicked, he walked over to where she rested. He planned to tell her that his fall was not some grand scheme of his, but then stopped just a step away. The sight of her delicately holding the bunch of tulips was yet another perfect picture that he wanted to forever hold in his mind. Yes, that is exactly how he would hold her in his memory long after they returned to the Garden of Ali Mardan and went their separate ways. In that moment, Lamar forgot all of his other thoughts as he looked at Zuli's elegance. He then scanned the Garden of Tulips; he sensed that his parents' spirits were close. He had felt them before, lovingly guiding him through his life of solitude.

The conversations Lamar had with his mother always inspired him. On one lazy afternoon his mother spoke to him about the unforeseen trials and pains of life, and the political mayhem that made life progressively more difficult.

"Every heart breaks. Every hope dims. Remember, my son, every leaf, once emerald green, falls with a fading beauty and is tread upon by passing feet. Flowers have thorns. A summer breeze turns into a wild, dark wind. The sapphire ocean offers pearls while drowning lives in its bosom. In the flames of death flickers a yearning for life. All trees and blossoms renew with offerings of hope. Beauty gracefully emerges from the dirt where its roots are bound. Every fate you will know is nothing but a test of faith. Every passing minute you will know is firmly rooted in miracles."

Through this, Lamar learned that, although life had its own unforeseen ups and downs, he had to remain optimistic and resilient to overcome despair.

Lamar would have loved to bring his mother to these fields so she could have picked tulips for the dinner table. She dutifully prepared food for her family without ever missing a day or meal. His mother was an excellent cook. She was known as the chef of the family, and was even quite popular among the entire community. How he missed his beloved mother, who at times was a tough guide and teacher. He realized that the degree of her pleasantry depended on the level of his misbehavior. To the best of her abilities, she fulfilled her motherly duties and made sure he learned the rules of life.

His thoughts went from the kind face of his mother to the face of the girl who slept serenely on the bed of tulips. She opened her eyes, looked right at him, and extended her arm to him. He knew what this gesture implied, so, with a firm grip, he grabbed her hand and helped her up. He made sure not to squeeze her fingers too hard, as she had done to him during their free fall off the cliff. Then again, she had clasped his hand so tightly that the pain of her squeeze had actually taken his mind away from the fall.

They walked together through the fields of ceaseless tulips. These gardens were of no particular dimensions or any geographic design known to Zuli – or anyone, for that matter. She looked at Lamar, who walked to her right, and saw that he, too, was captivated by what he witnessed. From a distance, these fields appeared to resemble silk Afghan carpets, the same carpets made by the impressive yet invisible hands of the faceless, nameless, resilient women and children of her beloved nation. These carpets covered the polished marble floors of Zuli's palace, with each room carefully color-coordinated much like the fields of tulips.

They weren't quite sure in which direction they moved. They saw nothing but glorious tulips. There were no birds, animals, bees, or bugs – nothing at all.

Lamar suggested that, as soon as they found an

opening in the fields, they should rest before the sun set. Zuli agreed to his suggestion and, soon after, they found the smallest landing where they could rest without crushing or breaking any more tulips. Because they lacked ample space, they were forced to share one spot, bringing them side by side. As night started to hover over them, they grew increasingly tired and fell into a deep sleep.

Zuli felt something softly brush against her face. An unfamiliar sound was very close to her ear. It almost resembled ocean waves, or the sound of a rushing river. Zuli knew that only she could have heard the brief, loud, and unusual sound – it was *that* close to her left ear. She looked up and saw the most exquisite butterfly flying at a slow, deliberate speed above her. She looked at Lamar to see if he noticed the butterfly, but he was fast asleep, facing her on his left side.

She moved a little closer to take a good look at this young man she was stuck with, who almost killed her yesterday by falling on her. She squinted against the already-risen sun, as bright as ever, to see more details of his face and overall body. He was good looking and very tall. Actually, the more she stared at him, the more handsome he appeared. He had a mysterious look about him that, at times, seemed very serious and brooding. Yet, at other times, he was easygoing and even funny. She was certainly funnier than he was, but that was only if she allowed herself to become friendlier with this stranger who claimed he had known her better than she even knew herself. Zuli decided to dig further into the matter to discover exactly what he meant by such a claim. How long ago could it have been? After all, she was only eighteen.

Besides, no one knew her as well as she knew herself, and she liked who she was.

"Are you enjoying what you're seeing?" Lamar's deep voice made her jump out of her skin. Zuli hadn't realized that he was awake while she stared at him. He must have been pretending to be asleep. That made her furious. He probably thought she actually enjoyed looking at him.

"I certainly am not enjoying anything. I was merely checking to see if you were still alive and breathing." *There, that should put him in his place*, she thought.

"Well, it looked to me like you were quite taken by my good looks and fully enjoyed such a long period of observation!"

"You're far from charming," she retorted. "I suggest you get up so that we can be on our way. And, mind you, we have a visitor."

Lamar looked upwards to see that she pointed to the circling butterfly. Awestruck, he rose to his feet, trying not to scare away their newfound company. The delicate insect had a very pretty face, much like an angel or a fairy of sorts. It was as dazzling as a colorful cloud under a thousand sunbeams. The butterfly had magnificent wings that resembled the finest pieces of Victorian china, covered with patterns and colors he had never before seen. It floated and whirled. It was a gentle and fragile creation: a silent beauty. Lamar had read about butterflies and remembered that some people viewed them as nature's fairies. Others saw them as short-lived creatures, symbolizing transient free-willed beauty, created to delight others. Lamar and Zuli watched the splendid butterfly swiftly fly around them, locking them in a full circle. It swooped down and landed on Zuli's left shoulder. Neither she nor Lamar dared to make any sudden moves. What happened next left them speechless and nailed to their spots amidst the fields of tulips. The butterfly spoke!

"Greetings to you, my lovely-as-ever Zuli. And salutations to you, Lamar; you are more handsome than before. Adir sent me to guide you. You both had the full pleasure of meeting my wise friend. He is, indeed, the wisest of all the wise.

You may call me Lilith, yes, that would be my name. Yes, yes, I can clearly see that you're both in complete shock, but snap out of it quickly, since we don't have much time on our hands! We have to get to Almaas and save it before it's too late.

"Who is Almaas, you ask?"

Actually, they had not asked. They hadn't spoken a word nor moved from their spot.

"Well," continued Lilith, "*Almaas*, as you know, means 'diamond'. It's the tulip with the silver roots, the one we must save if we want to preserve the whole Garden of Tulips. Come along, let's go, chop chop!" Without even looking back, Lilith rose from Zuli's left shoulder and flew into the air.

On their way, Lilith talked without the slightest break. Apparently, she loved to talk. This became increasingly obvious to Lamar and Zuli since, during their hike, neither was able to get a word in edgewise. As they watched Lilith's moves with ample delight, Lilith remained oblivious to her own beauty and flew with ease. She displayed a unique air of gracefulness, almost as if she didn't want to disturb the earth's atmosphere.

How very surprising it was to Lamar to watch such magnificence. She had a name, could talk, and had only flown by Zuli's left side, precisely parallel to her height, not even an inch higher or lower. Thus, each time Zuli turned to look at Lilith, they were always at eye level with one another. His mind stayed with this thought for a second before he noticed that the brilliant colors of Lilith's wings changed with each flutter. The colors never remained the same, changing from one shade to another, to yet another. It was a sight too rich even for his extraordinary imagination. Lamar's thoughts were cut short by Lilith continuing her one-sided conversation.

He heard Lilith say, "Now, do you remember what Adir warned you about?" Before they could answer, Lilith continued, "Of course you do. You're both very clever and bright in every sense.

"As I was saying before I interrupted myself, based on what Adir told you, we must be extra careful not to set foot on the fields of bleeding heart tulips. These tulips have the urge to destroy everything that crosses their path. Essentially, they suck the color from other tulips to give themselves more strength. You do know that the beauty, essence, and life expectancy of any flower or plant is naturally tied to its rich and lush appearance. Of course, you already knew that fact. It would be impossible for the two of you to cross so many fields without getting caught in the dangerous webs of these monstrous tulips. So, do either one of you have any plans for crossing the fields of bleeding heart tulips?"

Zuli watched Lamar open his mouth to express an idea that popped into his head, but he closed it without uttering even half a word.

Lilith had already moved on. "Of course you don't have a plan. How could you possibly know? Neither one of you have ever been here before. Well, good thing I'm here. In fact, it's the only reason I'm here: to specifically help you cross these fields without putting either of you at risk. You see, the goal is to ensure you are not harmed in any way so that you may travel onwards to your next destination. Did you know that I volunteered to guide you on this journey?"

Zuli and Lamar looked at her without attempting to answer. It was a good thing, too, because Lilith continued, "I'm looking forward to the three of us joining efforts and minds to find Almaas. Soon after we find it, we can leave these fields and the Garden of Tulips once and for all. Know that no matter how it appears to the eye, I shall be with you in spirit endlessly."

For a split second, there was a pause in Lilith's speech. She fluttered her colorful wings in a rhythmic dance, flying a bit to the right, then a tad to the left.

"I believe we're to go this way; our destination is east." After walking along what seemed like a short pathway, there was an archway of sorts overlooking yet another world of tulips. Fields upon fields were arranged with perfect order at the foot of another, side by side. The tulips danced in the open air just to please the scope and grasp of the eye.

Lilith did not speak a word during this time. She allowed them to take in the serene splendor of nature in their meditative states. They both knew that the image of the Garden of Tulips would remain with them for their lifetimes. Zuli wished she could take out her notebook to draw a quick sketch of the scene, but Lilith was already moving forward and expected them to follow. So they did just that.

They traversed through boundless fields, giddy from the fragrance filling their senses. After a long while, they found an opening to rest among the tulips until the first light of daybreak.

The next morning, the sun rose as if on fire. The first of its rays beamed down on Lamar's face and awoke him. He noticed that he was the first to wake; he had always been an early riser. In fact, he did not get much sleep, especially when the rest of the world was in their sleeping hours. He enjoyed the quiet and solitude of the evening, allowing him unity with his thoughts. Lamar also loved to read a variety of books, and was drawn to poetry, biographies of learned individuals, and histories involving the world of fine arts, literature, and classical music. Even as a young child, he would read with much deliberation and reflection. He took his sweet time to chew through words, analyze sentence structure, and churn verses in his mind long enough to actually taste their meanings. As he got older, he attempted to write his own short stories, research papers, and even composed poetry. The world of literature and art had a strong pull on him that considerably tightened its grip on his interests as he progressed in life.

Back in reality, Lamar stretched his entire body before getting up. He was careful not to make a sound or sudden movement to avoid disturbing Zuli, who was still asleep, and Lilith, who was comfortably resting on Zuli's shoulder. Lamar left the two sleeping beauties to inspect the area and see where their paths led. He had only walked up the path for minutes when he heard some sort of noise. It was more like something moving under the ground beneath his feet. He stopped to listen, but didn't hear anything. He took a few steps backward, to see if it came from behind him, when he suddenly felt a sharp, painful jab below the calf of his right leg. He jumped up, launched forward, and turned around in an abrupt manner.

Looking down, he saw that there was a small patch of ground with tulips resembling red hot peppers. He looked at the back of his excruciatingly painful leg with unease and, much to his surprise and relief, saw that he wasn't bleeding to death. Making sure to keep his distance, he stretched his neck, leaned over the red tulips, and peered around. The tulips that attacked him had open bulbs, ready in hopes of another strike. Right then, Lamar saw large, gruesome eyeballs, similar to human eyes, at the heart of the flowers' bulb. The sight made his skin crawl. If that wasn't bad enough, the tulips each had a set of fangs as sharp as knives protruding from their petals.

Lamar tried to comprehend such a phenomenon. He dashed around the tulips, sprinting toward Zuli and Lilith. They were totally unaware of their surroundings, still in a deep sleep, as if they had nowhere to go and nothing to do.

Lamar yelled at the top of his lungs, "For heaven's sake, wake up!" Zuli rose to her feet looking confused and flustered. Lamar then recounted everything that had just taken place. He even showed them the spot where he was attacked, where a red mark remained on his leg.

In a state of panic, he shouted, "With the two of you sleeping so deeply, I could've bled to death and you would've never known! It would've been too late!"

Zuli looked a little closer at his leg and said, "I don't even see a drop of blood on your leg. How could you have possibly bled to death? Stop being so melodramatic!"

Lilith ignored both of them, circling higher in the air before descending to Zuli's height, always on her left. She announced that they had arrived at the fields of bleeding heart tulips.

"You must watch your step from here on out. Be sure not to get too close to these particular red tulips."

Zuli and Lamar walked side by side, keeping close but deliberately ignoring one another. They both looked out for red tulips; whoever saw one first would warn the other to avoid any mishaps. Lamar even extended his hand to Zuli to help her go around a steep area. She said thank you, but, of course, refused his help. After all, she wanted him to see that she was capable of anything, more than he would ever know. At least his attempt to help her, he hoped, showed her that he was a bit of a gentleman, regardless of the fact that he did not live in a palace or grow up with a silver spoon or two in his mouth.

Lamar was amused by Zuli's open display of courage and stubbornness. He wished the same unbeatable courage for women from all walks of life within their society. Where he lived, most women were dominantly controlled by the forceful might of men. This negative influence was neither constructive nor fair. Lamar wished women had more freedom of choice, with louder and stronger voices to express themselves without fearing repercussions or dire consequences.

He grew up in a home where men and women were treated equally. His mother was the ruler of their home. Yet, he knew all too well that the majority of women who left the security of the four walls of their private domain were not guaranteed equal treatment. He knew that such injustice was the root of all maladies and failures for their entire nation, holding it back from becoming a more sovereign and independent homeland. How could a nation be self-governing and dynamic without the input of half of its population?

Lamar always viewed the women in his family, who had quite sturdy foundations, as strong pillars holding up their home. They were the ones who shaped their overall lives. He saw women as just as intelligent and hard-working as men. He even witnessed the heightened resilience and utmost tolerance of women within society when faced with harsher treatment. They never lost the will to continue supporting their families, regardless of the injustices committed against them by the domineering hands of men.

Of course, most of this was caused by a lack of proper education. A very high percentage of the population remained illiterate, with no access to proper schools and teachers. This, combined with the anguish of poverty, was a catastrophic recipe for a failed state. The results of this recipe could be found in many parts of the world, where destitution still prevailed.

Lamar decided to tell Zuli that she should be more involved with the empowerment of women in their nation, considering that she was the daughter of the king and the nation's young and talented princess. This gave her a strong platform to voice her opinions. She held a significant and effective position, allowing her to influence the minds and hearts of most, and close the gap between the two genders once and for all. When this gap was closed, it would eventually eradicate most of the harsh treatment of women and replace it with mutual respect. This was the essential seed that needed to be planted in order to reap perpetual harmony. Thus, Zuli and he were on this journey to find the fig blossom that offered such everlasting equality.

Through extensive global media coverage, Lamar was well aware of the world's fast-paced advancements. He thought to himself: *Just take a good look at the countless countries on the other side of the world. They thrive because of equal opportunities for men and women, regardless of color, creed, ethnicity, or religion. They are blessed with peace and joy. Our country could soon be just as blessed.*

Lamar would discuss these matters with Zuli as soon as she snapped out of her prolonged bad mood. He wondered when that would be. Any day now, he was hopeful that she would show a softer side towards him. She was not aware of this, but he was familiar with her kinder side when he used to watch her roaming Kabul's streets, disguised from the eyes of others. Except, of course, *he* knew it was her. He followed her to make sure she remained safe and returned to the palace unharmed.

Lamar's ponderings were interrupted when he noticed that Lilith had flown very high to check the area for any signs of Almaas the Tulip. They spent a few hours hiking up and down the paths, through bleeding heart tulips, trying to avoid Lamar's fate or worse. Lamar preferred to call them hot pepper tulips since he still felt the sting of one on the back of his leg. These flowers held an uncanny and eerie resemblance to human eyes devoid of all warmth. The eye, surrounded by dagger-like fangs, was clearly visible when the tulips' bulbs were open.

Even though they were wary of their surroundings, Lamar tried his best to encourage Zuli to pester the tulips with a stick he found so she could see them attack. She refused, telling him that he was acting juvenile, always looking for silly things to do. Lamar knew then that her mood would not lighten up anytime soon. Mostly, he did not appreciate her tone and rude comments in front of Lilith.

So he told her, "I have a better idea, Zuli: why don't you stick your whole arm in there? Then, you'll get to see the eye up close as well! It really doesn't hurt too much, give it a try why don't you? It might help the flow of blood to your heart!"

"Now, now," Lilith muttered. "Stop bickering, you two. How about being nice to one another? It takes a lot less effort. Besides, your entire journey is based on teamwork –"

Lilith interrupted herself with an elated shrill. "There, there's Almaas! See it? Can you two see it from where you're standing? No, no, come more towards me. Move more to that side and look all the way to the left. Do you see it now?"

Zuli gasped, "Wow! I've never seen anything like it!" There were fields of nothing but dried dirt ahead and a greenish black dust cloud loomed above the ground, giving everything a dim and wretched aura. Yet, in the middle of all the gloom, with not a single colorful tulip in sight, was the brightest of all lights. Its spot on the ground was luminous, as if one thousand and one stars were clustered under the blackest of night skies. The silver glow had sparkly undertones, similar to the rays of a high noon sun hitting the surface of the glistening water, bouncing the sunbeams back not in just one direction, but in all directions, as a mirror would. Almaas remained unaware of its own radiant brilliance, the only tulip left among the despair. Although the fields looked bare and arid, once they drew closer, they could see that the bleeding heart tulips were buried. Only the tips of the bulbs were visible.

When they passed by the tulips, their stems immediately grew taller, popping up from the ground. When Lamar saw the flowers, ready to attack, it reminded him of Zuli's prompt attacks on him. The difference was that her eyes were prettier than the tulips' eerie-looking ones, and she had a set of healthy teeth.

After taking the necessary precautions to traverse the fields, Lamar, Zuli, and Lilith safely reached Almaas the Tulip. The air around it was so bright they had to shield their eyes and squint the entire time. Lilith turned to Zuli and gave her a tender look.

"Thank you for letting me fly so close to your left, but never questioning it. The same goes to you, Lamar, who I could tell wondered why I only flew with Zuli during our time together."

She added, "Thank you for allowing me to rest on your shoulder, so close to your heart. You don't know it yet, Zuli, but you have the purest of all hearts, filled to the brim with love. Your heart is not filled with just any kind of love, though; this love is a gift bestowed upon you from the greatest Source, far beyond our reach."

She looked at Zuli and Lamar and said, "You must remember that the exceptional gift of love has been granted to everyone, but only a few special people know how to actually connect to this love that resides within the chambers of their hearts. However, those who cannot easily connect must be kindly steered in the just direction."

She looked to Zuli and said, "Your hearts are joined as one. However, only you, Zuli, could provide the inner vibrancy and power that I needed to pass on to Almaas. Know this: without your heartbeat and vigor, I would not have lasted this long, nor would we have been able to save Almaas as needed. You know that a butterfly is a transient beauty only to momentarily please the eye of the beholder. We are here, but fleeting at all times."

Zuli was left speechless, with a lump in her throat and tears blurring her vision. Before she could say anything, Lilith swooped down and gently fluttered her wings against her face: a kiss just for her. She then flew to Lamar.

She told him, "You're a brilliant young man who will keep on the path of greatness, so long as you don't lose hope and continue to fasten your eyes only on matters of quality, substance, and true love."

As she said the last words, she winked at him ever so slightly. Without saying another word, Lilith swiftly flew towards Almaas. Lilith was unexpectedly enveloped in the brilliant dazzle as she got closer to the glittering gleam. Almaas glowed from the petals, the stem, and from underneath the ground where the silver roots were planted. Lilith greeted Almaas by fluttering her wings, as she had done before. She then proceeded to fly in three full circles around the tulip before landing on the petals.

Lamar and Zuli stood side by side, mesmerized by the scene unfolding before their eyes. As Lilith sat in place, the colors of her wings began to drain; Almaas' color became more vibrant. This process took less than a minute or two. Almaas looked even more beautiful and fresh, manifesting the deepest and warmest shades of a fine ruby. The more colorful Almaas became, the paler and more drained Lilith seemed. As Lamar and Zuli watched, Lilith became more and more invisible, until she disappeared entirely from sight.

"Lilith? Lilith!" Zuli screamed her name over and over.

She and Lamar launched forward, almost on top of Almaas the Tulip, to save Lilith. They knew that it was too late; there was no sign of her. She gave all of her powers and loveliness to Almaas, becoming one with the tulip. Zuli openly sobbed and Lamar put a strong, comforting arm around her.

Dismayed, they knew that they would never again see Lilith, that most exquisite and talkative butterfly. They both remembered Lilith's comments earlier in the journey: "No matter how it appears to the eye, know that I shall be with you in spirit endlessly."

One by one, raindrops began to fall. Lamar dropped his arm from Zuli's shoulder to shield his eyes with both hands. Just as he looked at the sky, a downpour began. The sky reflected all the shades of colors. There were hundreds of arched rainbows everywhere, with no beginning and no end. Their entire surroundings were covered with nothing but rainbow glory. Even the two of them appeared as if someone had thrown a bucket of paint on them, much like in the Indian festival of Rangwali Holi, a carnival of colors. What happened next left them awestruck.

Thousands upon thousands of tulips sprang out of the barren fields. It was difficult for their eyes to take in such a magnitude of magic all at once. These new tulips attacked and conquered the fields of the bleeding heart tulips, destroying their very roots, bulbs, and stems with a fatal speed and force. More and more tulips, a mixture of all arrays of colors, kept popping up and filling the fields at a rhythmic speed. No blood-sucking tulip survived; all dissolved, dying in the kaleidoscopic display.

Zuli and Lamar could not see the fields' end, which grew into boundless seas in all four directions. This spectacle reminded Lamar of when he went to see fireworks with his family. The fireworks were beyond amazing, but what stuck with him after all these years was the finale. That scene involved hundreds of loud and dynamic firecrackers, covering the massiveness of the grand sky, while a symphony of sounds played overhead. Lamar saw the rate at which these tulips sprouted from the ground and spread over the entire space, just like the overhead lights of fireworks flourished and dazzled his creative mind's eye.

Zuli was devastated by losing Lilith, but was mesmerized by the incredible exhibition of tulips and rainbows. The showers of rainbows reached from the sky above to the ground below. The raindrops left them drenched to the skin, yet it was warm and pleasant. What happened next was just too far beyond anyone's expectation: butterflies began to rise from the fields.

A world of color, with wings as vast as an eagle's and as small as a dragonfly's, rose from the very spot Lilith had become one with Almaas the Tulip. These magnificent creatures rose towards the blue sky until all was covered with fluttering wings of color. Zuli and Lamar stood in bewilderment.

As they watched, nature's beauty triggered greater awareness within the core of their spirits. Zuli finally understood Saint Basil's proverb: *He who plants kindness gathers love.* She realized how humanity must willingly give towards the rebuilding and nurturing of its roots, for the sake of saving the future. She thought that her generation should be made aware of this important fact in order to save nature and preserve resources in the universe. At that moment, Zuli felt it her duty to spread this message to her countrymen to avoid further climate calamities. This was the responsibility of each individual. After all, did Lilith not sacrifice herself selflessly?

Chapter 4

The Garden of Lily Ponds

> "When you see love with all your heart, you shall find its echoes in the universe."
>
> ~ Rumi

As Lamar and Zuli continued their journey, Lilith's profound words echoed in the passageways of Zuli's mind. Their voyage had already taken them to mesmerizing gardens. Nature had awakened her spiritual awareness; it echoed love only to those with the ability to listen.

The voice of Adir, the rock, still rang in Zuli's ears. Adir told them to always head east. More or less, this was their direction a couple days ago. They walked past acres and acres of fields of tulips. The surreal image of the vast array of colorful tulips would always remain in their memories. The flowers' scented perfume lingered but, very slowly, began to fade from their senses.

Zuli realized that she felt more at ease with Lamar walking next to her, step after step on their fabulous journey. At times, she even found that his company was a source of comfort for her, repairing a gap within her inner core. It was difficult for her to quite understand the feelings that nagged her. There were times when Lamar was less charming, even though he believed otherwise, and she had subtle ways of letting him know. Needless to say, she knew that he did not find her subtle ways so subtle, but Zuli was not too troubled about his frame of mind. After all, it was not like they were the best of friends. She had only just met him when he pulled her through the trunk of the fig tree – who would ever believe her once she got a chance to retell this story? She did not think anyone would, except maybe the palace staff. Then again, they had no choice but to sit, listen, and agree with whatever she expressed. Nevertheless, even with the irony of their acquaintance leading to a very slow friendship, Lamar's chattiness and sudden quotations of poetry felt as though they were puzzle pieces that fit perfectly in the chambers of Zuli's heart, making her appreciate their epic journey at a deeper level than she had anticipated.

Even as a young child, Zuli recalled feeling a sense of unease, as though she were missing a part of her heart's core. She was a thinker; hence, she always looked for a hideaway to enjoy a few minutes of solitude. She spent time by herself and allowed her mind to wander into the realms of her imagination. She believed someone beyond her existence was always close, who listened to her inner thoughts and knew her fears.

When she was six years old, she had a favorite spot within the grand palace, where she lived with too many watchful eyes and too many helping hands guiding her every tiny step. In the early afternoons, after lunch was served and consumed, she was expected to take a nap before teatime. She loved teatime because she ate cake and biscuits with cold milk. At times, she was even allowed to have some tea, which, of course, first needed to cool off. Sometimes Gulnar, her nanny, would blow on it to cool it down faster. No matter what the rules were, Zuli found a way to break them. It made her feel empowered and in control. When Gulnar blew on the tea, it upset Zuli. She could have done that simple task herself.

Considering her rambunctious nature, Zuli was not fond of napping. She had many plans to enact, and time was of the essence, not to be wasted napping. During these times, Zuli made sure that she had an escape route. And she did just that – escaped right from under everyone's watchful eyes. On certain days, she preferred to stay indoors. She loved to sneak into the dining room, adjacent to the living room, only to sit on the floor beneath the dinner table. She was on the lookout to make sure that her grandfather, who gave her his utmost love and attention, had left the room.

Every day, he was served coffee. She watched him drink the very last drop from a small china cup. Once finished, he always turned the small cup upside down, placing it on the matching delicate saucer, decorated with dainty flowers and trimmings. She watched with fascinated eyes because, as he placed the cup upside down, it left a perfect brown ring on the small china saucer. When he retired to his room, he always bent down to place a kiss on her face. Soon after her grandfather left for his afternoon nap, she would pick up the fragile china cup and examine the perfect circle left on the saucer by the coffee stain. She then brought the saucer to her mouth and licked it. It always tasted too bitter, but she didn't mind; it made her feel very grown-up.

Zuli spent hours sitting under the dining room

table. She spent that time either making up stories in her head or admiring one of the thick, heavy books with leather covers and golden imprints that lined the dining room walls from one end to the other. She could not read the books, but loved turning the fine, wafer-thin pages one by one to look at the photos of birds, animals, machines, and an array of other interesting objects.

Of course, if given the chance, Zuli enjoyed the outdoors, where she was farther away from the palace grounds and closer to the service rooms. This was the only place where she could get away with extreme activities, like climbing the apple trees and the low roof of the maids' quarters. The palace walls and roof were too high, making them impossible to climb; otherwise, she would have been up there in no time. On these days, the cooks' and nannies' children would join her, and they would all play together, free of worries and constraints.

Only as Zuli grew older did she realize the true difference between their lives. This realization created a division between her and the palace help. They could never again play as children without the pressure of customary boundaries looming over their heads. Now that the children of the two extreme classes, the elite and the underprivileged, were older, they knew exactly which lines not to cross. It was a well-established rule that required no vocalization or justification. Soon, Zuli realized that the entire society outside the palace walls was a social hierarchy, where citizens were categorized based upon their wealth, social status, and occupation. Zuli recalled that, at the age of fifteen, she detested such labels. She had empathy and compassion for the less fortunate.

Hence, with the help of her loyal nanny, she disguised herself and escaped from the palace to be with the majority of the population on the dusty streets of Kabul. She enjoyed having the freedom to roam and seeing where actual lives were lived. These were the real people who lived their lives with nothing more than hope and self-empowerment. Later on, Zuli realized that most people did not have the necessary means to lift themselves out of poverty and into a life of comfort or some degree of leisure. Regardless, the Afghan people remained hopeful even under dire conditions and refused to accept defeat. She had utmost respect for their tenacious resilience.

Zuli did not dare tell anyone in her family that she was ashamed of her status. She saw that she had an abundance of goods while others on the streets had next to nothing. Specifically, when she saw beggars roving around with outstretched hands and looks of desperation, she was utterly saddened. She was well aware of how the hearts of Afghan women and men were filled with compassion. They were modest, courageous, and desired to live peacefully. Afghans were known for their unwavering hospitality and love for their land. Zuli was proud to be from such an impoverished nation filled with kind-hearted people from a rich history and heritage. She knew that the broken pieces could be mended with perseverance.

Zuli and Lamar were not sure how far they had traveled, but they had come to a point where no tulips were in sight. Zuli noticed she was walking ahead of Lamar, whose pace had slowed. Seeing him stare into the distance, she returned to focus on the reality of the present moment. Lamar caught up with her, and they stood side by side. Their eyes locked onto the view, perfectly painted by the gifted and lavish hands of nature. What they witnessed was another tunnel of color. This, however, was a tunnel made solely of one color: green. Lush, rich, green trees proudly stood tall, reaching far, far above. It seemed like the trees dared to reach and touch the blue of the sky.

They moved forward, keeping their gaze on the magnificence ahead. As they approached, they saw trees of the greenest color lining the walkway. They could see no sky through the lush thickness of the branches, which curved to make a tunnel. They walked the last stretch until they were farther into this bright tunnel of green leaves.

Lamar surveyed the leaves with enthusiasm. "Look, these leaves are shaped like hearts, stars, and diamonds!" He noticed many others with different angles, curves, and twists he could hardly identify.

Most glorious were the tree branches intertwined so effortlessly, existing in perfect unison. Each branch was interwoven within the innermost part of this green tunnel, as if meticulously braided by the hands of a weaver. No branch was left untouched or uncovered by the velvety leaves. They radiated an inexplicable luminescence and held such detail, as if drawn by a painter's precise brush, dipped in a forest of the richest oil paints. The scene paraded before their eyes, creating an ambience completely of its own.

They rested in the tunnel of jade, the color bouncing off Zuli's jet black hair. Lamar watched the color settle in the deepest parts of her eyes, as though her irises possessed this very shade, as opulent as their surroundings. Once again, Lamar made a note of this precise image of Zuli, immersed within his mind. As their journey progressed, he would add more of these perfect images of Zuli to a special part of his memory, sectioned off solely for her magnificence, to be preserved forever. All the while, she remained unaware of her natural allure.

Lamar continued to watch her from where he lounged, his long, lean legs stretched out in front of him. He rested against a tree trunk, just a few feet away from Zuli. She observed her surroundings and wrote in her notebook. He wondered what she always wrote in that little book. It was obvious that she described the splendor of their settings. He hoped that she also wrote in poetic verses about the majestic trees overhead that reached for the heavens with arms greener than green. Lamar feasted his eyes on the sight, taking deliberate, long glances at their environment, which resembled mountains of emeralds. He fondly remembered their beloved butterfly, Lilith, who told them to look for mounds of jade and emeralds. Back then, it was not clear to what exactly Lilith referred. Now, without a doubt, it was evident to them both.

Zuli and Lamar discussed the next day's journey and the tips Lilith shared. They were to arrive just before high noon at their next destination, which Lilith described as one of her favorite gardens of all. Zuli and Lamar were excited, taking their best guesses as to what could await.

Lamar looked into the distance. "Wouldn't it be divine if we went to a garden of butterflies next? After all, Lilith was a butterfly. Maybe that's why it's her favorite."

"Oh, Lamar, that sounds unbelievable! I can't even imagine how the fluttering beauty we witnessed in the Garden of Tulips could be magnified," exclaimed Zuli.

The next morning, the brightness and warmth of the early sunlight touched the chords of Mother Nature's heart. The effects of the green splendor that had enveloped them all night long were surreal. Zuli took a few minutes to gather her favorite leaves, tactfully placing each between the pages in her notebook. Lamar was selective and only collected those in the shape of hearts. He knew that, when the heart smiled, life was green. He placed a few of them inside the pleats of the delicate laces wrapped around the magical silver-tipped tree branch, delivered to him on the eve of his eighteenth birthday. Lamar had vigilantly carried the branch in his inner jacket pocket on this journey from the Garden of Ali Mardan.

Not long after reaching the end of the jade tunnel, they found themselves standing face to face with a wall. This wall had no beginning and no end. It was covered with the same green leaves and draped with exquisite flowers. They were not sure whether to go right or left, but forward was not an option; they would just walk right into the wall. As Lamar stood there, perplexed, Zuli was quick to point out that she knew what type of flowers draped the wall; it happened to be one of her favorite flowers.

She looked at Lamar and said, "I used to pick these flowers from the Garden of Ali Mardan and place them in a very special vase that sat by my bedroom window."

Lamar heard only half of what Zuli said; he thought she had become quite the chatterbox. He was more concerned about which direction they should choose. Zuli moved closer to the wall and took a deep breath, sighing with elation as she filled her senses with the unmistakable aroma.

Zuli cleared her throat and stated that the flowers were called "*Nargis* (daffodils) and they're..."

Lamar interrupted her, saying, "Yes, yes, I know what they are, Zuli. They're my favorite flowers too and were also my mother's favorite. In fact, she grew them in the back of our home against the far end of the garden. She had a perfect view of them from every corner of our home. For your information, this flower is most admired by poets. Therefore, it's known as *Narcissus Poeticus* or the poets' daffodils." Lamar noticed that Zuli looked irritated.

"*For your information*, Lamar, it's very rude to cut a lady off. I don't appreciate it. Just so you know, you should wait until someone is done speaking before inserting your thoughts."

Before Lamar could answer her, she went on, "Now, which way are we supposed to go? My feet are starting to hurt and it will get warmer as noon approaches."

As she finished speaking, she put one hand to her forehead, acting as though she were too hot and about to faint, while extending her left hand to brace herself against the wall for a minute's rest. While Lamar, amused, watched Zuli's melodramatic gestures, he saw her place her hand on the wall. In the blink of an eye, she fell out of sight. It took a few seconds for Lamar's brain to process what his eyes had witnessed, and then he realized that, not long ago, he himself fell right through the trunk of the fig tree that stood in the Garden of Ali Mardan. Lamar did not waste another second. He reached for the wall. Sure enough, his hand went right through. What he was not expecting was to be grabbed by another hand and pulled through the wall in the most sudden and unexpected fashion. The force of the pull was relatively strong, and he landed a few feet away from the wall.

Zuli looked down at him with a huge grin. "Welcome, welcome! I hope that you now understand how it feels when you throw people around as you did to me at the Garden of Ali Mardan. I clearly remember that you almost broke my arm when you pulled me through the trunk of the fig tree."

Lamar took one look at Zuli's satisfied grin. He extended his hand up to her, implying that now she should help him up. She hesitated for a split second, but obliged to his gesture with an air of smugness. She came close, bent down, and offered him a helping hand. As soon as Lamar got a good grip on her slender hand, he pulled her down so forcefully that she screamed, falling to his side. Part of her body hit him and the other hit the ground, raising dust around them. Lamar laughed proudly as he pulled himself up, throwing her his own smug look. He left her disheveled, lying on the ground. Lamar did not wait for Zuli to get up. In reality, he wanted to help her, but decided to enjoy the hilarious moment a bit longer. So he walked right past her, hearing her muttering a few choice words about him.

Lamar and Zuli moved forward on their path, leaving the green wall and tunnel behind. Their straight path came to a sudden right turn, then a small hill, followed by another sharp turn to the left that took them further up a larger hill. They could still see nothing but the path ahead. However, when they crested the hill, they saw a blue universe spread at their feet.

There were countless ponds, situated in all corners, each of different shapes and sizes. If that was not enough, the ponds' grandness was amplified by the most vibrant and unusual water lilies. Standing high on the hill and gazing with wonder, Lamar tenderly said, "Now we know exactly what Lilith meant when she told us that we would reach one of her favorite gardens." Lamar and Zuli had been led to Lilith's favorite garden on their search for the unseen fig blossom. They had arrived at the Garden of Lily Ponds.

The unexpected glistening vision of ponds amazed Zuli and Lamar as they gazed around, walking and observing the ponds. The spectacular bodies of water were in different shades of greenish blue and deep aqua. They had no idea that in these ponds lived thousands upon thousands of fish. Lilith had told them to find her friend Kasib, the fish, with a turquoise-colored head; he was to deliver them a message. However, they did not expect such a multitude of fish.

Lamar was overwhelmed by the pure splendor of nature that had been gifted to mankind. He was reminded of a verse he had once scribbled down in his notebook, where he wrote most of his poems: *A pure golden blessing is to see the soul of love on the faces and in the hearts of every human being in the garden of humanity.* He wrote these few verses one day when he roamed around The Garden of Ali Mardan and observed Zuli from hidden corners. He watched her as she picked a handful of flowers, and as she sat under the fig tree, which she always hugged as though hugging a friend. It was heart-wrenching for Lamar to know that, at times, mankind could not see nature as a gift from beyond. There was a lack of respect for the delicate relationship between man and nature. Hence, people remained oblivious to how the Almighty's love manifested itself within nature just for their joy.

Zuli lifted her right hand, held onto Lamar's forearm, and whispered, "Let's go that way; I don't want to disturb the fish in these ponds. They seem somewhat gloomy to me, but then again, I don't really know too much about fish and their moods."

Lamar looked at Zuli sideways and whispered back to her, "I'm shocked that you're not an expert about the different moods of fish. Don't you pretty much know everything?"

Zuli threw him a harsh look and replied, "Oh my, I'm shocked you would even question that notion because I know so much more than you, Lamar! Now stop talking and keep walking."

Lamar smiled. He thoroughly enjoyed teasing Zuli and provoking her sweet temper. He also enjoyed the way she still held his forearm. He felt the softness and warmth of her touch through his jacket and shirt, on his skin and up to his heart, making it beat faster and skip all over his chest. Lamar took a deep breath and hoped that she did not hear the loud pounding of his heart. He said, "Yes, let's go this way, Zuli," and they set off into the Garden of Lily Ponds.

Lamar thought of his dear mother. Sometimes she also held onto his arm with the tenderness of a mother's touch. He had never truly allowed his feelings to take him too deep into the pain of losing his mother. It was the kind of pain that the mind and body rejected simply to protect the heart of the mourner from breaking into a million pieces. At the time of his mother's passing, Lamar made a conscious decision not to cry even one teardrop. He thought that no mother should witness the tears and pains of a motherless child.

Demoralized, most Afghan children silently bore such pains in the cages of their broken hearts, either from losing their mothers or both parents at the ferocious hands of war. He was well aware of the high number of orphans in his war-torn country. He was also aware that decades of war left Afghanistan as one of the least developed countries in the world, with millions of orphaned children. However, Lamar no longer felt like a child. After all, he was a man of honor and responsibilities who buried two parents and lost nearly all of his family to either death or migration. Even before his twentieth birthday, Lamar saw himself as a man. He was ready, willing, and able to help build a better future for himself and all of those neglected and abused children. Once and for all, he hoped to eventually free his beloved homeland from the deadly grip of ethnic conflicts, which had been the cause of continuous warring between numerous Afghan tribes over specific ethnic lines and means of assimilation.

His mother had been a lively soul indeed. Lamar was well aware that his own innate wittiness and dynamic characteristics were traits his mother passed onto him. As he looked at the ponds, the sight of water glistening and dancing before his eyes reminded him of the summer days when his family packed various foods and drinks for lavish picnics. His parents owned a home in Paghman, where many families went to enjoy the gardens of fruit trees and the rolling grass fields. The Paghman River was fed snow-melted water from the surrounding mountains. The freshness of the air was welcoming since they were away from the hustle and bustle of polluted life in the capital, Kabul.

Everyone enjoyed the body of water that twisted around the rocks embedded in the river, where kids gathered under the watchful eyes of the adults. Lamar recalled watching his mother stroll down to the river. She would carefully choose a spot to sit on the rocks, soaking her tired feet in the chilly water rolling beneath her. She relished the water flowing, the tides drifting, and the currents glistening. Diamond droplets soared into the air just before plummeting toward the river's surface and sinking back into the tides, only to wind out of sight. Lamar took delight in savoring the fullness of the river as his mother sat daydreaming beneath the rays of light.

His mother was also a skilled entertainer. No matter where they went during summer breaks, Lamar's mother was a storyteller who recited poetry and acted out her tales. It was a one-person show, a solo performance that featured the musings of a comedian combined with the recitals of a poet and the talents of a creative storyteller. She fully captured the audience's attention, which consisted of Lamar's immediate family. At times when his mother was not the center of attention, the family called upon Lamar for their entertainment. Lamar did not mind being in the center of such gatherings – he too enjoyed making everyone laugh. He acted out dramatic stories, danced, and played different characters. The entire family would watch him, laughing and encouraging his improvised show. Lamar felt very lucky that, while growing up, he had had such a close relationship with his mother. However, he also put her through much aggravation by constantly using his overactive mind and breaking his parents' rules. Gazing at the ponds, he wished she could have seen this garden. She adored all of nature's bountiful beauty. His mother also rested in eternal peace, beside his father, within the seamless layers and folds of her beloved land.

Lamar fought back tears, vowing to visit his parents' resting place upon his return to the Garden of Ali Mardan. As always, he would pour fresh water and place his mother's favorite flower, daffodils, over their plots. He would pray and pray for their souls, and would definitely tell them about this enchanted journey. However, Lamar was aware that, whether he visited his parents' resting place or not, their spirits were with him, never apart. This much he knew without a flicker of doubt.

Lamar's preoccupied thoughts snapped back to the present when he felt Zuli tug his arm, guiding him onwards. He followed her and, finally, they found themselves in the center of all the lily ponds. Here, they had a clear view of each. He stood alongside Zuli, listening to her sporadic gasps as she set her eyes on random ponds and their wholesome beauty. They both knew all too well that The Garden of Lily Ponds would remain their most favorite of places. These ponds were of various shapes: hearts, rhombi, crescents, and many zig-zags. What Lamar witnessed from the high-top of the hill he now saw up-close. The tints and shades of the bodies of water were deep aqua, with tinges of green and sapphire.

Each pond was covered with water lilies. These had unusual colorings: greenish-yellow with inner blue petals. The most beautiful and prolific water lilies featured brilliant and intense shades. There were profound red flowers with bronze leaves as well as cup-shaped lilies with just a hint of indigo. The ponds also featured a variety of irises and lotuses, with diverse dark leaves providing a wonderful contrast to the blossoms. Never before had Lamar seen such an array of plants in different sizes. There were leaves as small as coins and as large as his imagination, if not larger. There were vibrant plants with straight or curled stems and spiky or feathered leaves. Some of the leaves arched outward and were topped with a sprout, forming a spectacular umbrella shape.

In spite of the overwhelming gorgeousness of the flowers with the grandeur of the ponds, the multitude of fish dazzled. Lamar thought the garden could have easily been called The Sea of Fish. They were of inconceivable shapes and colors, while some had distinguished, human-like features.

Bending to take a closer look, Lamar swore he saw a fish that looked just like one of his mother's good friends who regularly visited them at odd hours of the day. He had addressed her as great-aunt, and she loved to eat nothing but *aushak* (stuffed dumplings). Lamar giggled remembering an incident that got him in a lot of trouble. He had run into the house after his little cousin whom he always teased. He simply did not see his great-aunt's oversized pair of shoes on the floor, which caused him to trip. He lost his balance and went flying towards his great-aunt while she ate a full plate of stuffed dumplings. Needless to say, he was punished accordingly. As expected, his great-aunt went back to the same plate and finished whatever food was left.

Staring at the fish and laughing about his fall that day, a preoccupied Lamar turned to Zuli to show her the fish that resembled his great-aunt. He did not realize she was bent down at his side. Lamar's abrupt turn caused him to bump into Zuli's back, which made her lose her balance. Lamar heard a loud scream and an even louder splash.

"Oh no," he thought. "Now, I'm dead!"

Zuli had stopped to admire two-heart shaped ponds connected on each side by six spikes, like the points of stars. The pond was filled with an array of floating water lilies and plants. The pond was a masterpiece, if you will. She bent down to reach into the water to refresh her hands and face. She felt a push forward and belly flopped into the water with much force, making the loudest and biggest splash. As she floated down on the water's surface, thousands of tiny fish stopped all movement to simultaneously look up at her. Zuli's eyes popped out of their sockets, staring back at all those eyes. As she struggled to get up, she felt a hand at the back of her dress.

Lamar watched Zuli in the water for a second or two before he felt a gut-wrenching panic. Alarmed, he reached for the back of her dress, swiftly yanked her out of the water with one strong pull, and stood her upright on the ground in front of him. Zuli's face, hair, and clothes were soaking wet. There were leaves stuck to her head. She was furious and eyeballed Lamar, a puddle of water forming beneath her wet shoes. Yet, even drenched, Zuli still looked like fireballs were about to shoot from her eyes.

Lamar started to apologize for the unintended incident, but Zuli stepped away from him and yelled, "Lamar, you're an absolute monster, far from a gentleman! How dare you push me in like that? I could've very well drowned. Just look at my clothes!" She exclaimed, "You must respect me exactly as I should be respected. It's the law of the land, don't you understand?"

"I promise you that it was a complete accident," reassured Lamar.

Before he could say another word, she turned on one heel and marched off. She left a trail of water behind her as she went, still yelling, "I will not allow you to treat me like this. I will get you back for this, just you watch."

Lamar realized that Zuli was just fine. Aside from getting soaked, no harm had come to her from the fall. So he yelled back at her, "*Mohtarama* (Ladyship), with utmost apology, I have no choice but to remind your highness that it was an innocent accident. Nonetheless, I look forward to any paybacks from you with much eagerness, your ladyship.

"Besides, how could I forget? You've only been acting as if you're the most influential, the one and only princess.

"What can I do for you, your royalness? May I shine or wipe down your silk shoes? After all, I'm just a *moochy* (shoe repairer) at your service. Or would you like me to take your clothes and hang them from the tree branches, so they dry up super-fast, perhaps by fanning them myself? Tell me, which will it be, your majesty of all majesties?"

Zuli stopped in her tracks and turned around to face him. She retorted, "Just look at my dress! You've ruined it. By the way, you're not funny at all. Just keep away from me or I will hurt you, I promise.

"Oh, one more thing: what kind of a moochy would shine silk shoes?" Again, she turned on her wet heels and stormed off, picking leaves and other shrubbery from her dress and hair.

Lamar watched her storm off. A surge of mixed feelings came over him. He wanted to run after her and either give her a piece of his mind or hug her. Instead, he remained immobile and watched her with utmost adoration, overwhelmed in ways only he fully understood.

Zuli went to find a more private area to dry her clothes, away from the prying eyes of Lamar. The incident of her falling in such a startling manner reminded Zuli of the first time her father taught her to swim. Without hesitation, he threw her in the pool, which was at the back of the palace grounds, and told her to keep kicking. She remained underwater for a while until she began kicking to save her life. It turned out that was the effective, if not dangerous, way she learned to become a strong swimmer. Of course, Lamar had no idea that she was a good swimmer. Therefore, she could not wait to show off her skills if they ever swam in the ponds.

Lamar spent the night alone under a lemon tree situated between the ponds. The aroma of the lemons tickled his taste buds and made his mouth water. He decided to pick a few good ones; they tasted more sweet than bitter. Even the lemon peel tasted sweet, just like a lemon candy, so he ate that, too. The lemons probably would have tasted even sweeter if Zuli was with him. He could not bear being away from her. Oddly enough, he realized that he missed her even when they were together.

Zuli's whereabouts were a mystery to him. The last time he saw her was when she stormed off, drenched from the accidental fall into the pond. He felt it was necessary to give her space to cool off and would make it up to her later. After all, tomorrow was another day.

Tomorrow, a new day, came quickly. Lamar woke under the lemon tree, with bright neon lemons hanging overhead. He knew that he had to find Zuli, but before he found her, he would prepare a platter of fruit for her. He hoped that it would help ease the tension between them in the exquisite garden of water lilies, fish, and ponds. Lamar chose an exquisite plant that looked like a large fan. It had such an unusual color: deep purple with touches of white and peach around its outer edges. Lamar arranged some peeled lemons, a few cherries, and an apple he split in two, leaving one-half for Zuli and feasting on the other half. He sectioned a few small yet juicy tangerines and placed a whole pear in the middle of the plant. Further away from the lemon tree, he finished the platter off with daisies that opened to feel the sunrays' tilted warmth. Lamar chose daisies because they represented innocence and simplicity, attributes he adored in Zuli. The act of giving daisies to another person also symbolized a loyal love. Lamar was very pleased with his arrangement and he decided to present it to Zuli with a poetic verse. That would really put her in an excellent mood.

Lamar walked in the direction Zuli went yesterday, using both hands to carry the fruit platter so his arrangement would remain intact. After all, he realized that, around Zuli, he had become the biggest klutz ever. It took a while before he found her, in the same spot where she fell into the heart and star-shaped pond. She actually sat with her feet dangling inside the pond, making little splashes and giggling. Lamar called her name so that he would not startle her again. She looked towards his direction and waved. Lamar breathed a sigh of relief when she acknowledged him with a friendlier manner than he anticipated. He stopped next to her and realized that small fish were swimming around, over, and under her feet.

She looked up and smiled, "It's soothing yet ticklish at the same time; you should try it."

Lamar bent down and said, "I will, it looks like fun." He held the fruit arrangement with both hands in front of her. "Zuli, you don't know this yet, but I know without a doubt that the purity of your heart and beauty of your untouched soul is that of fine pearls from the ocean of love." He ended his sentence with a distinct smile. Zuli stared at him with a puzzled look as a shade of color rose into her cheeks. Lamar saw her blush. That was good enough for him, so before she could say anything to ruin the moment and his efforts, he brought the fruits closer to her and said, "Please feast on this since we have a challenge ahead of us."

She looked down at the delectable platter, taking it from him and uttering no word but *"Mamnoon!"* (grateful).

While Zuli enjoyed the fruit, Lamar sat next to her and put his feet into the water. The water was just the right temperature; the fish swam around his feet, tickling him. He felt totally relaxed and overjoyed that they were back to normal. They discussed the possibilities of how they were to find Lilith's fish friend, Kasib. It was in this most relaxing moment that Lamar felt something jab the bottom of his right foot, causing him to jump out of his skin and scream much louder than he wanted.

Perturbed, he pulled his feet from the water and, when Zuli saw Lamar's reaction, she too screamed and removed her feet from the pond.

"What? What is it?" she asked in a panicked voice.

Lamar was shaken, and shouted, "I don't know! It was something sharp! Why does this keep happening to me? I may have been bitten by something poisonous! What if it was a deadly poison? I think I feel its effects!"

At that precise second, they heard a husky voice. It

was the deepest male voice they had ever heard, and it came from inside the pond. "Please do stop your overreaction, Lamar, my friend from the Garden of Ali Mardan."

Zuli questioned, "Did you hear that?"

"Yes, of course I heard it! How could I have not?" snapped Lamar, in excruciating pain as he hopped on his uninjured foot. "Did the voice come from the pond?"

Zuli and Lamar, terrified as to what they might find, kept their distance from the pond's edge and peered into the water. What they saw was a fish with a pronounced grin on its face.

Zuli and Lamar breathed, "Oh, wow!" Zuli nervously returned the enormous grin with a faint smile; Lamar looked at the fish with a question mark plastered on his face.

Zuli cleared her throat before she asked, "Did you say something or is there someone else down there?"

The fish grinned even more, if that was possible. They both saw his full lips move to form the following words: "Yes, I spoke. No, there's no one else down here. Welcome to the Garden of Lily Ponds. I am Kasib, also known as the earner and provider. I earn trust and respect and, in return, I provide hope. My beautiful butterfly friend, Lilith, sent a message to alert me of your arrival before she..."

A shadow of sorrow passed over his face and he continued. "May she graciously emerge above all boundaries into a new light. What I wasn't expecting was such an elaborate entrance by you two into this pond yesterday." His eyes turned to Lamar as he said, "I do apologize, my young friend, for the jab to your foot, but that should be a reminder that you really should watch your step around these ponds. You don't want to fall into certain ponds because there are unfriendly fish that are always eager for fresh and enticing bait to munch on. Nonetheless, I am indeed charmed and honored to make both of your acquaintances."

Lamar and Zuli mumbled their hellos. Lamar put his right hand over his chest and slightly bowed. Zuli watched what Lamar did, a customary greeting among Afghan men. She was not sure what to do with herself, so she made an awkward curtsy, like those she had seen in movies. When Lamar saw what Zuli did, he could not help but chuckle to himself. Kasib looked at them with the same striking grin plastered on his fishy face. The range of colors on his body was most spectacular. Kasib the Fish had a glittering body, but if you looked closely enough, you could see that each scale was infused and gilded with specks of pure gold. This color harmonized with that of the fish's head, saturated with a rich and vibrant turquoise. His tail was a fiery orange that played between inflamed red velvet and dusky black, infused with dashes of pure white. His vivacious tail whirled with every movement and they watched Kasib maneuver through his underwater empire with purpose and ease.

Kasib went on to say, "Do you have any clue as to what your mission is within this grand garden?"

"Well, Lilith told us that we were to find you, and that you would inform us of the actual challenge we would face here," Zuli explained.

"Yes, very well then," responded Kasib. "Foremost, do you still have the magical fig tree branch with the silver tip? I do sincerely hope that you haven't dropped it somewhere, considering you're both accident-prone."

Lamar confirmed, "I assure you, Sir Kasib, I've guarded it with the utmost care."

"Excellent news. Please, you may address me as just Kasib. The task at hand is a burdensome undertaking of utmost importance. You see, this garden is the most magnificent of all gardens because it encompasses not only all flowers and plants, but also the entire animal kingdom. At one time, everything lived in harmony. The majority of the citizens in this garden were the diverse families of fish. If the fish could not exist in total contentment, this garden would not be able to endure the current brutality of captivity and encasement. It would gradually wither away. This problem we face is caused by *Shahbanu Sanam* (beautiful queen)."

Lamar chuckled and repeated, "Shahbanu Sanam – is that her real name?"

"I would not make fun of anything related to Queen Sanam if I were you, Lamar."

Lamar uttered an apology as Kasib continued, "Queen Sanam is the leader of this entire garden. Her name is a symbol of love and beauty, yet she ruthlessly rules. She governs with an iron fin, if you will. By commanding all of the pond gates to be locked down, she took the freedom and liberty of travelling from countless fish. Many fish families have been locked behind gates, unable to even visit each other. These gates were once open, allowing all to swim anywhere they pleased." Kasib narrowed his blue and green eyes and looked from Lamar's face to Zuli's before adding, "From your personal experiences, you both know all too well of the damaging results a nation suffers from repressive and despotic governance, Lamar especially."

Before Lamar could comment, Zuli interrupted him. "Mind you, I too understand. My father, the King, has done his best to bring peace to the country he loves more than he loves himself. Peace cannot be attained when a country is at war with itself, and when its citizens are unwilling to join hands in unity for the betterment of their future. Sooner or later, everything begins to cave in and completely collapses beyond repair. This is the truth of the matter. This is why Lamar and I are on our journey to find the magical fig blossom."

Kasib exaggeratedly nodded in agreement and said he would be right back. He swung around his tail and disappeared deep into the water. Lamar and Zuli knelt on their hands and knees at the edge of the pond in an effort to see Kasib. They could not see too well since he swam very deep into the pond. All they could see was the reflection of their own faces on the water's smooth, paling façade.

In addition to the gorgeous water lilies floating on the crest of the water, there appeared to be hundreds of tiny eyes of smaller fish just below the surface. Their color palette was a harmonious marigold, roseate, and magenta. When Kasib reappeared, the score of fish disappeared. Kasib did not lose momentum and explained, "Do pardon my sudden departure. I had to run water through my gills for some much needed oxygen. Now, where was I?

"Oh yes, one day, when you are queen of your own land, I know you shall govern first from the heart and then from the head. The simplest trick to success is to empower one and all fairly and equally, knowing that everyone and everything has been created with the seeds of integrity, morality, and righteousness.

"However, sometimes we lose our way, much like Queen Sanam. The queen was born to very handsome parents. Contrary to her parents' good looks, let's just say, she sadly lacks certain welcoming features. It's imperative that you two remind her that *zaibaee* (beauty) comes from within the heart and not from perfectly chiseled outer features.

"There are times in different stages of life when we must voluntarily take it upon ourselves to help others, even if help is not asked for."

"Exactly how are we supposed to achieve that? Perhaps we could use one of our wishes to inspire Shahbanu Sanam to change. After all, we have a total of three wishes," Lamar mentioned to Kasib.

"No, no," Kasib mumbled, shaking his head. "Your mission is to retrieve the most unique lotus flower from the deepest pond. You'll use one of your wishes to help you achieve this task. The wish will allow you to freely swim among the fish and you will never need oxygen, whether you stay above the surface or swim to the bottom of the deepest pond, where this lotus is planted.

"As you may know, this unique, elegant flower is a symbol of hope and purity. The lotus has had roots embedded in the pond's floor for thousands of years.

The stem grows tall enough for the flower to sit atop the surface of the water. The flower is more sweet and tasty than all of the world's candies combined.

"However, when you pull it out of the soil, make sure the roots stay intact so it can regrow for another thousand years. You will then offer the lotus flower to Queen Sanam. If the queen eats the flower, we're all doomed. If she decides to share it, the dark cloud will forever vanish from the Garden of Lily Ponds. I know it's a lot to take in, but you two are more than capable.

"In essence, this task will help you with your search for the magical, never-before-seen fig blossom. You have the remainder of the day and evening to discuss this and ensure you understand your roles and responsibilities.

"You can roam the ponds, but stay away from the west side of the garden, where the unfriendly fish await. Lastly, you must make your wish at precisely midnight. You will then be granted access to the ponds, and I will simultaneously gain the ability to stay on dry ground for no more than twenty-four hours. Please remember that; otherwise, we will all instantly suffocate." Kasib smiled even wider and added, "I don't wish to suffocate on dry land because my gold scales will surely melt under the sun. We shall meet at midnight." With those last words, he vanished into the depths of the pond.

Lamar and Zuli picked themselves up from the side of the pond and decided to tour the divine garden together. The more they wandered, the more hypnotized they were by the exquisite panorama. This was indeed a colorful journey that no one would ever believe. They stopped at some fruit trees, where Lamar picked the best-looking ones, offering the sweetest fruits to Zuli, who ate and ate. The berries stained her lips with a deep red hue. Zuli kept the simple white daisies Lamar had given her earlier in the day as part of the fruit platter. She took the stem of one of the cherries and tied it around the flowers, making a small bouquet. She then placed her delicate accessory behind her left ear. It framed her face perfectly, the white petals resting against the deep black of her hair. She looked like a true empress of love. Lamar had to peel his eyes from her beauty. He did not want her to notice that he was completely taken aback by her naiveté and sophisticated charisma. It was at this very second that Lamar realized he was totally in love with Zuli.

He said a little prayer under his breath: "Oh, dear God, help me." In that moment he experienced the most petrifying emotion. In order to get his mind off his unsettling condition, Lamar suggested that they venture to the west side of the garden, much against Kasib's clear warning. Lamar assured Zuli that he would not do anything risky. It was part of his nature to be curious and he was eager to see what the dangerous fish looked like.

"Come on, Zuli, I've seen how very curious and adventurous you can be. What do you say? Are you in?" Zuli could not pass up the challenge, so she agreed. Of course, leave it to Lamar and his brilliant ideas. He suggested they fill their pockets with only sour lemons to feed the fish and see their reaction to the bitterness.

Walking westwards, they saw amazing life in the near and far corners of the garden. They were greeted by an assortment of colorful dragonflies, swans, ostriches, and very, very far away, they could make out giraffes, zebras, and other mighty animals. As Lamar predicted, they had an exhilarating time finding the ponds with the dangerous fish. These fish were hostile and had gloomy combinations of colors. They sped to the surface to see if they could bite Lamar's long arm, outstretched high above the water, dropping in pieces of lemon. The fish did not miss a beat; they attacked and guzzled the lemon pieces. Their faces twisted and contorted beyond their naturally hideous looks, making Lamar and Zuli laugh. Some of these fish even jumped high into the air when Lamar held up the lemons. Zuli told him that he could lose a finger or two if he kept that up, so he finally stopped.

At eleven minutes to midnight, both Lamar and Zuli paced back and forth awaiting Kasib's arrival. Lamar held the magical tree branch with the silver tip, still wrapped in layers of lace. They heard the sound of water rippling as Kasib appeared from the depths.

"Greetings," he said. "Shall we begin?" Both Lamar and Zuli nodded in affirmation. "Please unwrap the tree branch, hold it in the center of the three of us, and point the silver tip straight down towards the pond," Kasib instructed. "Now, together, please repeat after me. The first enchantment is: *O' let a fish on unfamiliar land form a new bond. Let the mortals breathe through the water under the pond.*"

Lamar expected something to happen. Maybe he would grow fins and gills. Both mortals waited to see if the sky would turn black or if Kasib would grow legs. Still, nothing unusual happened.

Lamar looked down at Kasib still in the water and said, "I don't think the wish worked. Shall we try it again?"

"Oh, it has worked," replied Kasib. "Which one of you would like to get in the pond first? As soon as you do, I shall be transported to your place on land."

Zuli put her hand up and said, "I will do it." She sat on the edge of the pond, and then looked up at Lamar for reassurance. Encouraging her, he nodded, and she tentatively lowered herself into neck-deep water. She was face to face with Kasib, who smiled at her ever so widely. The next second, he stood on two fins next to Lamar at the edge of the pond.

"Oh my!" shouted Lamar and Zuli. Kasib looked like a tiny shrimp next to the tall and strong Lamar. At that point, Lamar knelt down and extended his hand as if he wanted to shake hands with Kasib. Zuli could not believe her eyes when Kasib grabbed Lamar's huge hand with both fins and shook it. It was then she noticed her countless colorful visitors. She was surrounded by scores of fish. They were all smiling at her, or so it seemed. She now swam on her back, fish covering her. Giggling jubilantly, she yelled, "Look Lamar! Look at me!" Lamar and Kasib turned to look at Zuli swimming on her back. Instantly, Lamar's jaw dropped and he could have sworn he had a slight heart-attack.

Zuli was covered in exotic colors as if she wore a ball gown made of all the flowers in the Garden of Lily Ponds. Kasib looked at Lamar's face and saw Lamar entranced by Zuli's exquisite beauty in the water.

Kasib marveled, "Zuli you're the most beautiful princess. Lamar, are you not going to go in the water? Go ahead, acclimate yourself. Some of the fish are your guides and will show you around for the next couple of hours.

"You will then have until sunrise to rest under the lemon trees. At that time, you must swim with the same fish guides to retrieve the lotus flower, which has black seeds and red and green petals. While you two are busy touring the ponds for the next two hours, I will visit a few old friends and savor some fruits. We will meet here at sunrise."

At first both Lamar and Zuli were hesitant to swim underwater in case the wish did not work. But, the extraordinary acts that took place right before their eyes dawned on them. Kasib the Fish walked on dry land, eating fruits and visiting old friends. Lamar took Zuli's hand and down they went into the clear blue. They were now fully part of the aquatic scene, the water inducing an absolute calm over them. Zuli waited for Lamar to take the first breath, and Lamar expected the same from Zuli. Both were hesitant to put all their trust in a magical wish.

With one last meaningful look into each other's eyes, Zuli and Lamar took deep breaths. Ironically, they held their breaths in anticipation for the worst, but all was good. Neither had bulging eyes, a purple face, nor suffocated from lack of oxygen. Lamar exhaled a great sigh of relief. This caused a cloud of bubbles to rise and Zuli was taken over by giggles. They were both soon convulsing in laughter, the water playing with their hair and the fish swimming precariously around the two strangers to marine life. The water was neither cold nor warm, and felt welcoming and rich against their skin. The ponds' floors were gardens in their own right. The beauty of the coral reefs, rocks, and other exotic marine life were beyond their wildest dreams. The fish led Lamar and Zuli from one pond to the next. They could only go so far, however, because at every point, they faced cage-like gates designed to bar direct access between the ponds.

Although they were having fun in the water, Lamar and Zuli knew they had to rest before the next day's challenge. Swimming back towards the main pond, Zuli dared Lamar to race her. Lamar did not think twice and agreed. The school of fish parted to give them ample room for their competition. The guide fish became referees for the race. Lamar was much taller and stronger than Zuli, but she was a skilled and determined swimmer who knew the proper techniques. When the race began, Lamar was ahead at first and smiled to himself, seeing the end of the pond approaching fast. But he was tired and thankful the race would end in his favor. That was when he saw a slender figure with wavy black hair effortlessly glide past him. He lost his concentration and was even more fatigued, his arms and legs out of sync.

Needless to say, Zuli won the race. She waited for Lamar to reach the end of the pond and smiled proudly.

She teasingly jibed, "There, I got you back so good!"

"Yes, indeed. You won fair and square," Lamar panted.

Zuli and Lamar were exhausted after their swim

with the fish. Zuli fell asleep under the lemon tree just a few feet from Lamar. He stayed awake, considering the day's delightful events. He decided tonight would be the night to take Zuli's notebook, without her permission, and write her a letter. After all, tomorrow would be a busy day, and soon after they accomplished their goal, they would head east.

After Lamar finished the letter, he placed three jade, heart-shaped leaves he had saved from the tunnel of green trees inside her notebook.

The Love Letter

Princess Zuli, dearest to my heart,

As you roamed the streets of Kabul, I, as your protector, roamed just a step away, guarding you at all times. I watched you among all others and realized that there was a thousand-mile gap between you and all of the girls I saw. If you recall, I told you at our first meeting in the Garden of Ali Mardan that I have known you all my life. I was once told by my grandfather that we each have soulmates in this vast world. The lucky ones find their soulmates, while the less fortunate ones continue to search indefinitely.

A few years ago, when I was just a little boy, you appeared on the canvas of my mind as a new draft of the face I had seen before in the mirror of my soul. This was way, way back in time, when I was in the garden where our fig tree stands, resilient and strong. Then and there, I knew that you were the one. After all, you are noor (light). Ask yourself, what would the sun be without its radiating glints of light? It would be nothing but a dark orb. It is only I who can clearly marvel at your shine while you remain unaware of your effects upon my world. Now I see beauty at dawn and dusk, and experience joy and love everywhere in between.

I want you to know that I will never ever betray your trust in me, and please never forget that I, Lamar, would rather die than hurt you in any way. I believe that true love is without walls and can be found within our interlocked hearts. Our circumstances and backgrounds are quite different; you are the future queen of the land, and I, just a humble citizen at your service. As fate would have it, our paths are two opposites, never to cross at an intersection where I may be able to earn your love. Remember, we will only be separated by a footpath from our garden. But, my lovely love of my life, know that you will never be apart from the shores of my heart. Love in its true sense must be selfless.

I write while you sleep soundly under the lemon trees and bright stars in the Garden of Lily Ponds. You will see these words in your notebook, learning that I love you with a full heart. I shall never see myself apart from you; our hearts shall always be connected. I hope that we at least remain friends by the strings of our souls — far, but never apart. I will always carry the memories of our colorful and legendary journey between my heartbeats. If I could, I would jump in each pond to collect all of the water lilies just to lay them at your feet.

I have confidence that together we can find the mystical fig blossom to help us bring everlasting peace to our motherland. I hope that you, too, will cherish the memories of our exceptionally amazing journey within the depths of your heart. In the meantime, you are locked within the cages of my own. The key is under the deepest pond of lilies, and the lock is sealed with a kiss.

Yours,

Lamar

Soon after sunrise, Zuli and Lamar met Kasib at their usual water lily pond. They found Kasib eating some cherries. Zuli and Lamar gasped in bewilderment at the sight of their friend walking back and forth, casually eating an assortment of fruit. As they approached Kasib, he greeted them with one of his especially elongated smiles. He shared a few extra details with them, and reminded them how they would be guided to the deepest point of the pond.

Kasib observed them both. "You will have no trouble finding the lotus flower since it has distinct dried black seeds and exceptional red and green petals. It rests alone, positioned regally in the center of the pond's heart. It is protected by fish guards who have been alerted and are awaiting your arrival."

He continued to say that, as soon as they retrieved the flower, the guides would direct them to where Queen Sanam resided. Kasib would then meet them at the Queen's palace at eleven minutes past eleven o'clock, at which time the lotus flower would be offered to Queen Sanam.

"Now listen carefully," said Kasib. "If you face any trouble, the guides will be ready and willing to protect you. Remember that you can use the pebbles which you, Zuli, gathered after Adir, the rock, appeared. Those pebbles you've carried in your pocket are magical. They will become anything that you wish upon. You could even eat them, if you desired."

"Eat rocks?" Zuli asked in a curious tone.

"Yes, indeed. Should you ever decide to eat one of those tiny pebbles, first think of your favorite flavor and you should taste that instantly."

"Oh, I will be trying that without a doubt," affirmed Lamar.

Kasib went on, "For that matter, hold a pebble and think of any item, perhaps a painting illustrated by Monet that resembles this very pond. He happens to be one of my favorite artists. You shall then instantly hold an exquisite Monet painting. His paintings give distinct eminence to the water lilies within the ponds." Upon completing his informative statement, Kasib wished them both the best of luck as he swished away.

Lamar and Zuli swam between the fish guards. These fish were quite dangerous, with sharp and pronounced muzzles that could have cut right through another fish or severed a predator's limbs. Their double-edged tails were curved and had a sharp tip, like swords from the era of the Mongolian warrior, Genghis Khan. Their fins were like shields protecting them on each side. The score of fish swimming ahead helped push the current out of the way, making it much smoother and faster for Zuli and Lamar to swim.

They made several stops to observe the marine life. There was no shortage of vibrant jewels in this deep blue world, foreign to the entire population of Lamar's country. After all, Afghanistan was landlocked, leaving everyone without direct access to the sea. It saddened him to think that the majority would never see the greatness of an ocean. People had minimal access to rivers, ponds, or lakes. Lamar recalled the shortage of water during the scorching summers that caused rivers and wells to dry up. Most people had their own private wells in their yards. There were also public wells, far and near, where people formed lines and had no choice but to wait and fill their buckets. Younger kids were often tasked with this chore, and they could barely lift the heavy buckets off the ground.

At some point, Lamar realized they made a sharp turn heading towards another pond. To their surprise, this pond was not barred by the same gates they had passed for the last couple of hours. The leader of the guide fish swam between Lamar and Zuli, directing them to veer around an enormous coral reef. Neither of them saw any plants, flowers, or rocks ahead. All that could be seen was the guide fish circling around a flower's stem. They had arrived at the pond where the thousand-year-old lotus was rooted.

Zuli reached out, tapped Lamar on his shoulder, pointed to the lone stem extending to the surface of the pond, and remarked, "It looks like we've arrived." The stem was affixed at the center of the pond's floor, a great depth below.

Catching a glimpse of this elongated stem ahead, Lamar and Zuli were consumed by a sudden and unexpected wave. It threw them in opposite directions with an uncontrollable momentum. The guard fish began to gather in an unusual fashion. They congregated in one area, far from the two swimmers. When Lamar turned to see where they went, he faced the most frightening creature he had ever seen. A gigantic pufferfish zoomed toward them. Its whole body was rigid in permanent attack mode. Its spikes were fully extended and surrounded its massive, round figure. Lamar looked to see if Zuli was safe in the immediate unfolding of such sudden events. She was just behind him; together, they watched a war unfold between the fish and the giant.

Countless fish were either consumed or ripped to shreds by this massive, ferocious power. It speared at least twenty of the guards at once, swallowed them all whole, and spit out the remaining bones. Zuli then remembered Kasib's instructions. She reached inside her inner pocket and fumbled with its zipper until she was able to reach the pebbles she gathered from the Garden of Ali Mardan. Silently, she motioned to Lamar and handed him one of the pebbles. Lamar then swam to the other side of the fight, further behind the giant. Meanwhile, Zuli swam to the opposite side. Together, they threw the pebbles at the giant fish. They imagined the rocks were explosives. As they did so, the score of guide fish withdrew, swimming away from the predator. There was a huge explosion as the pebbles came in contact with the attacker. Such an abrupt reverberation caused the predator to deflate and flee. The whole team breathed a sigh of relief.

They continued to swim to the center of the pond, towards the thousand-year-old lotus flower. Zuli followed the original plan exactly as it was described. She would swim to the surface and Lamar would stay at the bottom of the pond. He was to make sure the thousand-year-old roots stayed intact. As a result, the lotus flower would regrow for another thousand years, waiting for a new generation facing a different mission. Zuli whirled and swam in powerful strides to the surface of the water, where she saw the blue of the clear sky and the brightness of the sun beaming down. The guard fish did not want to risk another attack, so half of them swam with Zuli, encircling her. The rest stayed with Lamar at the bottom. To her surprise, reaching the lotus flower and pulling it out required no effort. Zuli handled it with meticulous precision, holding the beautiful lotus with one hand and pulling upwards. It broke off from the stem with natural ease. The roots remained in place, and the stem stood strong.

The pond where Queen Sanam resided was impeccable and striking, with innumerable rainbow fish. They had dual fins with an array of shimmery scales running from gill to tail. There were coral reefs of all varieties, with colorful rocks and sea gems. Brilliant white pearls floated everywhere around them. It was breathtaking, until they caught sight of Queen Sanam. *Lord have mercy*, thought Lamar.

Lamar gawked at Queen Sanam. Every fish he had seen thus far was quite beautiful. Even the notorious pufferfish had an interesting air. Poor Queen Sanam was quite hideous. Her head was too small for her body. She had black pupils with red centers, resembling sushi rolls. They were topped off with eyelashes like the dry ends of old corn pulled off the stalk. She had extra-large lips that barely covered her enormous, jagged teeth. The queen was larger than any other fish in the pond. Her scaly body was a dull orange color with no warmth. Her fins were covered with slimy bumps and were disproportionately small.

Lamar swam closer to Zuli and whispered, "My dear Zuli, you forgot to tell me you had a twin sister!"

Zuli threw him a killer look and blew as many water bubbles as she could muster straight at his face. She then retorted, "There, that should clear up your foggy brain, Lamar. Shouldn't you pay attention to what Kasib is saying?"

Lamar could not help but chuckle to himself as he listened to Kasib addressing the Queen.

Kasib looked even smaller in front of the gigantic Queen Sanam. However, his voice was still deep and commanding. "May we approach you, my Queen?"

The Queen spoke with a high-pitched voice, "What is your business here? Why did you ask for my presence, Kasib? You know very well that I have a full schedule on my fins. You are also aware that you are forbidden to cross the ponds. You have already broken too many rules."

Kasib cleared his throat and said, "Forgive me, my Queen. I believe you would be pleased to know that our guests are here. They risked their lives to retrieve that one remarkably special flower. As you know, only Princess Zuli and Sir Lamar were ordained to fulfill this task.

"They are the ones chosen to find the fig blossom. Princess Zuli is ready to approach and present you with the most delectable gift ever given. I am pleased to tell you, my Queen, that our guests must depart soon for their next mission to find the fig blossom and return to Adir. They are doing so to bestow peace and harmony on their war-ravaged country."

Kasib cleared his throat again and said, "My wise Queen, look around you. You have locked down the ponds, separating families of fish from one another. The Garden of Lily Ponds suffers from the bottom up, affecting all lives. Time is of the essence before this heavenly garden wastes away under a curtain of sorrow.

"The citizens of this garden are hopeful that you will remember the days when your parents reigned with love and respect. Dear Queen Sanam, may our guests approach?"

The Queen eyeballed Zuli and Lamar. She nodded and commandingly screeched, "Approach." They swam up until they were stopped by the queen's guards.

The Queen continued to glare at them, then locked eyes with Zuli and asked, "What is the state of your country and fellow citizens?" It was the last question Zuli expected to hear.

Thus, Zuli was caught off guard for a few seconds before regaining her composure, with help from Lamar's supportive arm on her shoulder. "With all due respect, as you know, I am the daughter of the King. My father is devoted to improving the well-being of his citizens.

"Unfortunately, our country has suffered endless years of war, caused not only by our own erroneous and flawed tactics, but also by the hands of our enemies, who continue to play shrewd political games.

"For many generations, this has brought an entire region of the world nothing but irreversible damage and destruction. This is why we were chosen to embark on our voyage to find the fig blossom."

"Yes, I see," said the Queen. "That is also the reason you were chosen to retrieve the lotus flower. We have been waiting for you for a thousand years. You have finally arrived; it's about time.

"Don't be afraid. Come closer. Where is the lotus flower? It is time for me to hold it with my own fins."

Zuli and Lamar swam closer to the queen, until they were face-to-face. At that time, Kasib bellowed, "We gather here today to witness an astonishing moment. As you know, I am *Kasib*, also known as the earner and provider. I earn trust and respect and, in return, I provide hope. I ask you, all families of fish who have congregated here, to witness our Queen Sanam as she is given the rare delectable lotus flower.

"She will either receive it with kindheartedness bestowed upon her by her beloved parents, the former king and queen, or she will reach for it just to eat it. My Queen, it is the duty bequeathed upon me by your father, the King, to let you know that if you consume the lotus flower by yourself, the curtain of doom will never be lifted, the cages and gates will not open, and the Garden of Lily Ponds will dry up and cease to exist."

Lamar noticed that the Queen's eyes bulged even more, if that was at all possible. Lamar said a prayer under his breath, and Zuli reached to unzip her pocket, looking deeply into the Queen's eyes.

"As I hold this flower, I know that true beauty blooms from our roots. Hence, the roots of this lotus flower remain intact in the heart of the pond. Only with inner serenity and love can one peacefully lead," Zuli said. She held the lotus flower in her hands and extended her arms upwards to Queen Sanam. She wasted no time, snatched it from Zuli's outstretched grasp, and brought the flower to her face. There was an instantaneous loud gasp from the families of fish, a rightful gasp of horror. As they watched, the Queen closed her eyes and brought the flower closer to her nose, which was nothing but two tiny holes, and took a deep breath to inhale its superb perfume.

Then, she looked at Zuli and Lamar. She said, "I admire your good deeds. I admire your hunger to bring peace and harmony to your country. I admire that you risked your lives to bring this to me, and your innate ability to see only the beauty of one's heart and soul. Hence, you have brought the lotus flower today. Foremost, I highly honor the memory of my parents and their good deeds." With these spoken words, the Queen separated just one petal and offered it to Kasib.

The cheers of a thousand fish erupted so loudly that Lamar and Zuli had to cover their ears. The deafening sound resembled an orchestra of flutes. The entire pond was filled with tiny bubbles popping everywhere. The sound of gates opening could be heard near and far. Newly-freed fish swam about. Kasib's smile stretched from one side of his face to the back of his head. Even Lamar and Zuli hugged and kissed one another three times on alternating cheeks, a customary greeting among Afghans.

Later, they stood at the edge of the hearts and stars pond and observed. The Garden of Lily Ponds looked brighter. There were greener trees and livelier flowers glowing from every corner. The animals and birds were roaming around, dynamically perkier. The bodies of water radiated blue tones as countless multicolored fish swam freely, causing endless ripples of aesthetic brilliance.

Kasib turned to Zuli and Lamar, saying, "It is time

for us to say our farewells. You shall be immensely missed, but we will meet again. Now, I am honored to introduce to you my very good friend, Mr. Matek."

Chapter 5

The Garden of Roses

> "The world has become peaceful for both the tiger and the deer."
>
> ~Rabia Balkhi

The pair turned to look where Kasib pointed with his petite fin. They expected to meet yet another fish, or perhaps a human, with the name Mr. Matek. When they turned around, however, there stood a stately horse. The horse locked eyes with Zuli and, in the most dignified manner, bent his right knee, lowered his strong neck, and bowed to her. A gasp escaped Zuli. Lamar looked at her, assuming she was scared by the size and height of the horse. Instead, she regarded the horse with an air of perplexed familiarity.

In a hushed voice, Lamar asked, "What is it, Zuli?"

As if Zuli did not even hear, she muttered to herself, "Oh my heavens."

"What is it? Will you please tell me?" Lamar demanded.

Zuli looked up at Lamar. "Lamar, you will not believe it."

Lamar responded without hesitation, "Try me. Just tell me, will you?"

Zuli gave him one of her disapproving looks and continued, "I know this horse from my dreams."

"Okay, now you're hallucinating," Lamar said incredulously. He looked to Kasib for some male bonding, but saw Kasib in agreement with Zuli.

"Ever since I can remember, whenever I fell asleep under the fig tree at the Garden of Ali Mardan, I dreamed of this very horse coming into the garden from a faraway distance," she said. "There were many times in my dreams that I rode this horse with considerable speed. We would gallop and jump all around the garden, as though we were on an obstacle course."

The regal horse then straightened, towering above the ground. Kasib nodded and said, "Yes, Zuli, you are right about your dreams. As you may know, *Matek* means 'gift'. Today, he is honored to be at your service, a phenomenal gift by all means. He is eager to take both of you from the Garden of Lily Ponds onward." Zuli did not move from where she stood, eyes still locked with Mr. Matek. Once again, Zuli curtsied, this time with precision and fondness.

Lamar looked at Kasib and asked, "May I approach it? I apologize. I meant to say, may I approach Mr. Matek?"

Kasib replied, "By all means, Lamar, he is a good friend of yours, too. You both watched over Zuli in the Garden of Ali Mardan. Mr. Matek, you do remember Lord Lamar?"

The horse turned towards Lamar and bowed his head ever so slightly. Kasib continued, "The only difference is that you and Mr. Matek were separated by realms."

Zuli interjected, "What do you mean, dear Kasib, that they were separated by realms?"

"You see, princess Zuli, imagine a considerably enormous yet delicate veil separating two rooms from each other; these are the outer and inner rooms, if you will. The veil is a representation of the time intervals that connect the spheres between our world and yours. I am certain that you, Lamar, recall being told about this very fact by your grandfather."

Lamar nodded, transfixed by Kasib's wisdom. "Yes, I distinctly remember. I had no clue what he meant then, but now I understand, without a shadow of a doubt. In other words, Zuli and I were destined to be connected from the very beginning of our souls' formations," Lamar said. "Our souls are bound in tight knots, yet separated by an invisible, delicate veil. Only those with inner stillness and an evolved soul remain connected, regardless of the veil, through endless passages of time."

Lamar took a few steps toward Mr. Matek. He put his right hand on his chest and bowed his head as a form of greeting and reverence, common among Afghan men. Once again, Mr. Matek bowed his long neck, this time more deeply. Lamar moved closer to the horse and began to stroke his pristine midnight black neck and torso.

Lamar remembered how proud his father had been to own several stallions. Although Lamar was raised around horses, he had never seen such magnificence. Nothing came close to the beauty of Mr. Matek. This horse was an impressive animal with undeniable intelligence and stature. *He is so handsome*, thought Lamar. He had never seen such a gallant animal, decorated with a sheer white mane that draped its neck like a fine adornment. This pure white mane covered his massive neck like silk dipped in a river of pearls. His imposing physique and strong legs seemed more powerful than one hundred of the toughest knights in shining armor. Long ago, Lamar's father told him a horse's tail was the most beautiful part of its build, unlike any other equids. Mr. Matek's elongated tail was luxurious to one's sight and touch. It almost resembled Zuli's flowing black hair in the water as she swam past Lamar in the lily pond and beat him in the swim race. Since the rest of his body was the blackest of black, the white of his mane was exaggerated against his dark frame. The splendid animal fascinated all eyes and hearts who beheld him.

Zuli and Lamar redirected their attention to Kasib, who spoke in his deepest voice. "I hate to end this heartwarming moment, but we have only a few minutes before the strike of noon. I do not wish to get deep fried on land by the beaming sun. It is imperative that I return to the ponds and assist Queen Sanam with her duties to bring vital stability and tranquility through a new set of laws, some that even the Queen herself cannot break."

Zuli and Lamar walked with Kasib to the lily pond shaped like hearts and stars. There was a somber and unusual silence between them. They knew they must say farewell forever. It was disheartening to watch tiny Kasib walk next to the tall Lamar, both with dour presences. Lamar could not help noticing how solemn Kasib looked. He knew they would never meet again.

Lamar chimed in to break the deafening silence.

"Dear Kasib, if you ever visit your wise friend Adir,

lutfan (please) do call upon us. We would be happy to show you around our city, Kabul. I will take you to my favorite spot in Paghman where the freshest water flows in the river, and gardens are lined with countless cherry trees, among many others. *Lutfan* promise you will." Though they knew the truth of the matter, they agreed to see each other again.

Zuli held Kasib in a warm embrace, refusing to let go. Lamar had to pull her away so Kasib could reenter the water before the spell wore off. They stood at the edge of the pond and watched Kasib mold into the depths, followed by a score of fish, until he was out of sight.

Mr. Matek waited for them until they stopped staring at the lily pond in hopes of Kasib's return. Both Lamar and Zuli gasped in unison upon seeing Mr. Matek, as regal as before, but now with an amazing carriage attached to his strong body. The carriage was beyond magnificent; it was fit only for kings and queens.

Mr. Matek himself resembled a knight, snatched from the heart of the night's blackness. Lamar was especially drawn to the horse's black and white palette. He once read that the color white allowed all other colors to surface at their full potential, while forming endless shades and tones. The color black covered all ills and faults from sight, but not one's internal flaws. However, Lamar saw that Mr. Matek had neither ills nor faults, and together the mixture of both colors was nothing less than stunning.

Lamar looked at Zuli, who stared wide-eyed at the carriage, and remarked, "This must be just for you,

Princess Zuli."

Zuli responded, "No, Lamar, this is for both of us. Do not forget: you're not so shabby yourself. After all, you are the son and grandson of noblemen."

Lamar stood to one side of the carriage and extended his hand to Zuli. At that moment, he was a true gentleman; Zuli placed her hand in his.

"Your ladyship," he said, "please allow me to accompany you on a carriage ride through the gardens of your dreams."

Zuli giggled and stepped into the carriage, maintaining a tender grip on Lamar's supportive hand. Once Zuli and Lamar took their seats inside the dreamlike carriage, Mr. Matek headed east, taking grand strides. Mr. Matek lifted his hooves one at a time, walking at a four-beat gait as his strong legs followed their normal sequence. He picked up his left hind leg, left front leg, right hind leg, and right front leg in a regular four count beat.

"You see, Zuli, I know a lot about horses since I spent ample time riding with my father. During our time together, he taught me everything that his father had taught him about horses," Lamar said.

Zuli looked at Lamar next to her, just a bit too close for comfort. Leisurely, he stretched his long legs in the spacious carriage. He was tan from spending time swimming under the sun. Once again, she was quite taken by his handsome looks and wavy long hair. Mostly, she loved the sound of his deep voice and the fact that, for a young man, he was articulate and had a hunger for life and wisdom. Yes, what she appreciated most about him was his caring heart, filled with compassion and empathy. Lamar was not aware of this, but Zuli was quite conscious of the way he gazed at her, and how his admiring warm eyes followed her from corner to corner. She made sure he did not know, but she actually enjoyed his subtle style and unique etiquette.

Zuli was guarded and conservative when it came to men's intentions. She grew up in a society that did not allow young girls to freely express themselves. This had an exaggerated impact on women to become more conservative than what seemed natural or necessary. Her mother, the Queen, was overly protective and strict. If she ever found out that Zuli disguised herself as a boy and roamed the streets of Kabul on a bike, Zuli would probably be locked up in her room until the end of time. Her father, the King, was a bit more lenient. He encouraged her to talk with young men to learn of their views and nature. Once, he even told Zuli to take her time in choosing her future husband. He emphasized the importance of discerning a person's characteristics, upbringing, and kind-heartedness before ever deciding to marry. Her father was against forced marriages and utterly disgusted by hearing of underage girls married off to older men for monetary and other inconceivable reasons. He was determined to pass yet another law to ensure that girls of all ages were protected, and Zuli wholeheartedly agreed with him. She deplored the idea of fathers, brothers, and other male relatives discarding young girls' wishes, physical safety, and mental health. They did so by putting girls in harm's way: in the hands of men lacking any sort of moral compass.

Her father shared with her information regarding

the role of a man in relation to a woman. He explained the universal teachings of the Holy Books, each text of a different religion, yet their creeds carried the same views and values. They detailed how a woman was created from a man in the most equal of senses, from next to the heart. God created a woman from a man's rib to always be permanently protected, never to be walked on or deemed unequal. Father and daughter agreed strict laws and necessary guidance were needed to protect the female population.

Then, Lamar, who was sitting next to her, asked, "What are you thinking about so seriously, Zuli?"

"Oh, I was just thinking about a few issues I must discuss with my father when I get back to the palace." Zuli changed the subject. "So, how do you like this enchanting carriage? If one could call it a carriage."

It looked more like an elongated boat. The carriage had two pointed ends that curled in an upwards fashion. The vessel's interior was even whiter than its exterior. The comfortable seats were suspended high, so Lamar and Zuli enjoyed the view from every angle.

Prior to embarking upon this leg of their journey, Mr. Matek gave them the opportunity to observe the dreamlike vessel he led. The carriage had eight wheels and only six of the wheels rested on the ground. The two others were off the ground, tucked underneath the carriage. The unique art on the wheels resembled tangled writings from languages spoken around the world. They could distinguish eastern alphabets of Farsi and Arabic with Hebrew, Sanskrit, and more. If they had time, they would have spent hours deciphering the words; perhaps there were hidden messages on the pure white wheels. Each spoke was engraved with intricate curls and loops. The wheels were fastened by shiny bolts and bejeweled with rhinestones.

What astonished Lamar and Zuli most was the stark white interior of the carriage itself. Every inch was covered with pearls of different sizes and shapes. It appeared as though someone had collected all the free-floating pearls from Queen Sanam's underwater palace. Zuli flashed a radiant smile and could not refrain from touching them. The pearls were affixed to the coach with delicate precision, which added much flair to the vessel. Lamar wished to take some of those pearls to design a beautiful necklace for Zuli.

He was reminded of a poem by Baidel: *The smile on your lips plays like a wave on pearls...the breeze in your hair fooling around as a devil in mayhem.* Instead of quoting the poem aloud, Lamar asked if Zuli liked pearls.

She nodded, "I truly like the feel and simplicity of pearls. I have a necklace passed down to me from my grandmother. It's the only one I like to wear, especially when I have to attend formal gatherings. To be quite honest, I don't wear much jewelry, only a few pieces that have special meaning to me."

Lamar listened intently, making mental notes. One day, perhaps, he would make something for her with his own hands. After all, he was an artist. Just then, he had a brilliant idea. *That's it*, he said to himself, *I will save part of my salary to buy some gold-plated nuggets and pure gold wires to make a necklace.* He would use the materials to make a replica of the mystical tree in the Garden of Ali Mardan. Lamar smiled, proud of his brilliant idea. He knew that she would wear it and never part with it since the meaning would resonate with her.

Mr. Matek galloped onwards, knowing which way to go. He never missed a turn. Zuli and Lamar observed more of the Garden of Lily Ponds since their eastern path ran through its center.

After some time, they left the ponds behind them. For two days they traveled through meadows, up hills, between grand mountains, and down steep valleys. The most spectacular sight was the plethora of birds, none of which were familiar to the two companions. Even Zuli, who happened to be an expert in many uncommon and outlandish matters, could not recognize the myriad of birds of all sizes and feathers. The stretch of fields looked like a grand painting hanging in midair under the bluest spread of sapphire across the ether, all for the pleasure of the observer.

Zuli realized she thoroughly enjoyed Lamar's every story, poem, and comment. She was drawn to people who spoke of substantial matters rather than frivolous ones, which bored her. She especially enjoyed Lamar's sense of humor since it matched hers. Everyone who knew her was aware of her caring and humorous nature. Of course, she guarded herself by not letting Lamar see that side of her. She needed more time to study the young man, who had already suffered at the cruel hands of time and circumstance. He walked strong and proud, yet his heart was broken into many fractions, spread in all directions. How very painful it must have been to experience the loss of both parents. He carried their memories within the tight grip of his soul.

On their journey from the Garden of Ali Mardan to the Garden of Tulips, Lamar had recounted his life story to Zuli. She was touched by how much he had already endured. Although she wanted to maintain her tough image, she did not hold back her tears while he told the story of his young sister. Lamar had to stop several times during the account as he became overwhelmed by the pain of losing his younger sibling.

"Zuli, I wish you had met my beautiful sister, who actually had some of your attributes. One could even go so far as to say she had a saintly soul. Her heart was no less than a golden orb. Her aura exuded light, while her eyes, sapphire blue, radiated warmth and love.

"Ironically, such a blissful heart suffered from a condition untreatable in Kabul due to lack of proper medical necessities. My father sold whatever valuables he owned to afford a trip abroad for her heart surgery.

"It seemed her fate was predetermined. The doctors could not save her, and she died in the arms of the man who loved her above all. He returned home with my little sister in a casket."

Zuli reached out and squeezed Lamar's hand with affection.

"My father was broken. He never recovered from the untimely death of his little girl, whom he adored and cherished. The loss of a child is shattering and offers no solace or respite. My parents suffered in silence, yet the memories of wailing and the sound of their hearts breaking have never left me.

"I proudly carry my little sister's memories. We were the best of playmates and got along very well. She remains an angel who frequents my dream, and she rests with my parents."

Earlier, Lamar noticed Zuli's melancholy after parting with Kasib. Lamar decided to tell her a funny story just to make her laugh. He loved the sound of her laughter – it was musical.

"Oh yes, Zuli, let me tell you about an infamous day full of rule-breaking and overconfidence. You see, my father warned me over and over to never take any of the horses beyond the grounds of our home without an adult's supervision.

"Of course, when you're eleven-years-old, you have the ability to listen, only to hear everything the wrong way. Backwards, that is! Just so you know, *my* young brain cells forcefully interpreted the rules differently than they were stated. I planned for my friends from school to meet me by the busiest street, in *chahar-raahi Haji Yaqoub* (the intersection of Haji Yaqoub), in *Shar-e-Naw* (New City), where we lived. With luck, all of us had managed to escape from home during the expected nap time.

"When I saw a group of my friends coming up the street, I walked towards them with my head held high, holding the reins of a colossal horse. Then, I had a brilliant idea. Instead of giving each of my friends a separate ride, I decided to have all three get on the horse for one ride together.

"With much difficulty and no help, I got the third person on. I proceeded to get myself on the horse, right up front, closest to its neck. I was trying to show off my horse-riding skills. Mind you, everything was going well as we paraded down the street, four people piled up on the horse. Now are you imagining this or not?"

Zuli was already giggling and could only manage to nod in affirmation.

"All was going well. Everyone admired us. We felt so cool, as if we were on top of the world. Since we lived in that neighborhood, most of the shopkeepers knew of our families. At some point, I was waving back to the *qasaab* (butcher) where we bought our daily meat. What I didn't expect was a loud car honk. The few hoodlums inside started driving too close to the horse to harass us. Well, the loud, repetitive honking transformed the horse's calm demeanor into that of a wild horse on a mission. The horse bucked, his two front legs going as high as possible.

"I dove, grabbed his entire neck, and realized two of my friends were no longer behind me; only one held me with a death grip. Let's just say I had the feeling the horse wanted to rid himself of both of us. He started erratically speeding down the road, and then the horse left the main road onto the sidewalk. I heard people screaming *'Pasho! Pasho! Kay asp aamad!'* ('Move! Move! A horse is coming!') Multitudes of fruit and pastry platters flew up in the air. At that point, I could no longer feel my friend's skinny arms and I realized I was alone on the horse. It was such a lonely moment! And the worst was yet to come, Zuli," Lamar emphasized. "The horse knew exactly which way to go and dashed straight to my house. There were scores of people running behind us yelling obscenities. I saw my house with the gate wide open: lo and behold, there was my father. At that precise moment, I wanted to release the horse and drop out of sight for good. But life is precious, so I held on, not knowing that my father was waiting to end it for me."

Lamar watched Zuli dissolve in laughter, crying through her cackles.

"A crowd of people, the horse, and I ended up by the house where my father stood, his fury palpable, emanating into the air. The minute the horse saw my father, even he stopped in his tracks. I'll spare you the details of my never-ending grounding and scolding." By then, Zuli and Lamar were unable to control their laughter.

Lamar then attempted to describe the sounds of Mr. Matek's hooves to Zuli. As the horse galloped and danced his way forward, his hooves played musical notes of all sorts, depending on whether he was going over gravel or more solid surfaces. Lamar heard the beats of intricate drum sets. There were also conga drums, combined with the jingles of several tambourines, mixed in with his favorite of all, the unmistakable tones and tunes of the tabla. Zuli listened to Lamar's passionate style of describing what he heard; all the while, exceptional scenes were unfolding before them. Along their breathtaking path, scores of birds greeted them as they traveled through fields, knolls, between imposing mountains, and down sudden steep valleys. Zuli and Lamar enjoyed watching the colorful birds against the everlasting bright blue sky. It reminded them of the azure skies of their homeland.

The multitudes of vibrant birds resembled the magnificent skies of Kabul when they were filled with the serenity of kites. Indeed, it was a sight beyond all sights. There were times when Zuli biked through the few parks and many back streets of different neighborhoods just to observe the many *kaaghaz paraan* (kites) that flew from the rooftops, street corners, or far away in the parks, avoiding many trees. From time to time, they would get stuck on the highest branches. Kids were left with little hope for the kite's safe return. After trying to free their kites from the trees, they always returned home with a shredded mess of paper, a kite destroyed. She loved the kites, handmade and attached to different tinted strings as sharp as a blade's edge, designed to cut right through one's flesh and the opponent's kite. She endured this bloody and painful experience for the sake of kite-flying. As a matter of fact, kite-flying was enjoyed by all ages. Adults participated with their own gigantic kites, while young children flew tiny ones. They shared the same space, on the ground and in the air.

At the palace, she used to watch the cook's son make his own kite with special string. When Zuli was younger and allowed to play with the servants' children, she helped with the kite-making projects and was known among the kids as quite a skilled flyer. How fitting that she then recalled a quote her mother loved by Anaïs Nin: *Throw your dreams into space like a kite, and you do not know what it will bring back, a new life, a new friend, a new love, a new country.*

Finally, Mr. Matek stopped at an intersection. From where Zuli and Lamar sat in the carriage, it wasn't clear what he was looking for. He made a wide and deliberate right turn, stopping at the foot of a waterfall. A humming sound filled the air from the tumble of water plunging into a clear pool. In it, the beauty of the high mountain was reflected, bouncing back into the air.

As soon as his two passengers departed, Mr. Matek moved forward a few steps, until he was at the water's edge. He took a long drink of the crystal clear liquid. Lamar could see that the sun was preparing to dip down, and Zuli looked for a good location for the night's rest. They decided on a spot between the waterfall and countless marigold bushes surrounding a grove of golden weeping willows. The trees reached sky high, yet drooped to their feet. The branches looked like gold chains with neither beginning nor end. Their brilliant yellow twigs were covered by blossoms and resembled wisteria florets. To the human eye, it looked like gold trickled down the branches, giving the impression of sparkling rain. It pelted down, dazzling and covering all. A soft wind stirred from one tree to the next, causing the sweeping branches to gently sway. Lamar watched Zuli's hair, caressed by the wind, dance in the air. He asked Zuli if she could hear the sound of the wind. He watched as she closed her eyes and paid close attention to the sounds of nature.

"Yes, I can," she said, "It sounds like a muffled flute." Lamar replied, "Yes, it sounds like a *nay* (reed flute). Do you know what they call the sound of the wind that has surrounded us, Zuli?"

She shook her head, "To my chagrin, I don't know. I'm sure if I think a bit more I will remember the word."

Lamar smiled at Zuli and retaliated, "Oh, no need to think too much, *azizam* (my dear), I will gladly tell you. It's a word that you've heard of many times: *hafifah*. It describes the sounds of the wind dancing through the trees."

"Oh, how fitting and glorious," Zuli exclaimed. She lifted her arms and danced in a circular motion, the winds carrying her words. "Lamar, Rumi once said, 'O sweet wind passing over lover's grass, blow in my direction, for the fragrance of love is my wish.'"

They stood still and allowed the wind to play with their senses, warmly acknowledging their presence.

Zuli missed being home; she loved that the city of Kabul was surrounded by mountains. While Lamar rested, Zuli watched the immense amounts of water falling from the peak of a faraway mountain. The water pounded onto the rocks below, creating an enticing silvery pool. Under the moon's gaze, the waterfall looked like a wall of shimmering silver and gold coins; it bounced off the shiny rocks into the darkness of the night. The relaxing sounds of the waterfall, with its power, urged Zuli to write in her notebook: *Yes, be a waterfall; erode and wash away the sharp, nasty edges of corruption, all while remaining true to the beauty of nature.*

It had been days since Zuli had a few minutes to herself. She had not been able to write or draw in her notebook at all. She took out the book and flipped through the pages, smiling at the memories she would carry back home. Much to her surprise, she thought she saw two unfamiliar pages. She flipped back and, to her sheer amazement, it was a letter addressed to her. She flipped to the next page to see who it was from.

Needless to say, Zuli did not sleep too soundly after reading and re-reading the love letter. The letter was written immaculately by the hands of a young man, her companion on an entranced journey. She lost count of how many times she read Lamar's letter pledging his love to her. What she knew for sure was that, each time she read it, his pledge sank deeper and deeper into her soul. This opened a window that allowed her to see beyond her thoughts, deeper into her heart.

"Oh, my goodness," she murmured to herself. She sat on a smooth rock by the pool of water, away from where Lamar was fast asleep under the looming willow tree. It was at this precise moment, under the watchful eyes of the rotund moon, that she felt herself fall. Her heart felt it might leap out of her chest, and her eyes were overwhelmed with tears of joy. It became apparent to her that she was spiraling outside of her usual self-control. She had fallen in love with Lamar.

She decided not to react at all. She needed more time to process this peculiar, yet delightful, feeling. She wished her father were close so she could tell him. For now, she knew that, with some deliberation and reflection, she would decipher her thoughts to help pinpoint her next move. Without making a sound, she walked back to where Lamar slept. Zuli fell asleep with her notebook held tightly in both hands, close to her heart; she made sure it did not get too far from her reach.

As always, Lamar woke up at the first blush of dawn. He saw Zuli lying a few feet away, to the right of the willow. He found it odd that she held her notebook, hugging it as if it attempted to escape. It only took another second before a wave of shock surged through him. She must have seen his love letter, written on the pages of her personal notebook.

"What have I done now? She will definitely never speak to me again," he muttered to himself.

Mr. Matek waited for them to board the lush carriage that morning. Never before had Lamar felt so nervous. At the same time, he had never seen Zuli so chipper and warm, either. One could even say she was being quite charming. Today, he decided to listen more and say less. He had a bad feeling that her cheerfulness would lead to him being chastised for the improper love letter. Lamar listened to Zuli and watched her exaggerated gesticulations, the movement of her full eyebrows, and her smile appear and disappear.

"Lamar? Hello, Lamar? Have you heard a word I've spoken so far?" Zuli asked.

He replied, "Yes, of course, Zuli! I have not missed one word yet. Go ahead and test me. I can recite it all, word for word."

"No need for that, as long as you're listening, because I'm concerned," she said. "It is a legitimate question you've voiced before. I don't know what our next challenge is or how we will find out. It's quite obvious Kasib had discussed our predetermined challenge with Mr. Matek, whose sole appointment was to ensure that we reach the next destination."

Suddenly, Zuli and Lamar stopped talking. Mr. Matek had gained momentum and was going faster and faster. The carriage moved from side to side in a reckless manner, gaining intense speed. Mr. Matek's legs galloped at such an alarming rate that he became a blur. Zuli peeked over the side of the carriage and saw that, with each of his forceful bounds, they began to practically hover over the marshy earth.

Up ahead, they saw a deep chasm approaching, one with an endless drop. Its bottom was so far down that all that could be seen was a pit of darkness. The whole ravine was lined with jagged rocks that could slice any object to pieces. Zuli and Lamar began to panic; it seemed impossible for Mr. Matek to jump over such a stretch of emptiness. Then, they heard a low mechanical buzz. Lamar and Zuli saw that two extra wheels were descending from the carriage's mid-section.

Hopefully these are to soften the landing, they thought to themselves. Nothing was going to stop Mr. Matek on his path closer and closer to the ravine's edge. Its opening taunted the two adventurers like the mouth of a large monster waiting to swallow its next victim. Zuli and Lamar were huddled close together. Lamar squeezed her even closer, his arms wrapped around her shoulders in consolation. They felt a rush of energy; it was Mr. Matek making that final jump.

Zuli's heart sank into her stomach at the thought of plummeting hundreds of feet downwards into the abyss. Just then, they felt leverage, almost like a cushion had enveloped the carriage. Lamar and Zuli tentatively looked with panic-stricken eyes to see that he had now sprouted two delicate white wings! In their incredulous state, Zuli and Lamar looked closer. They saw that Mr. Matek had not in fact turned into a pegasus. His supposed wings were composed of thousands of doves, all flying in unison to propel him forward. To ensure there was enough thrust and throttle, the larger doves utilized their extended wingspans to guide him left and right. Mr. Matek was in control as he executed a smooth landing. They had arrived at the Garden of Roses.

Lamar hopped out of the carriage as soon as it came to a full stop. He sprinted to the other side and offered both hands to Zuli to help her step down. He wanted to be a gentleman, but she was always too quick and would playfully jump out of the carriage before he could be of assistance. She hesitated for just a split second, looked into his eyes, and placed both hands in his.

Laughing, she said, "Catch me, Lamar!" She bounced off the carriage, letting go of his hands.

Lamar had to take a few steps back. "I got you, Zuli!" he said as he caught her, firmly locked in his embrace. It was a surreal moment, having her in his arms and against his heart. When Lamar looked into her eyes, so close to his, he knew he had the love of his life secured right where she belonged: with him.

Zuli felt Lamar catch her and pull her close. She found herself in his embrace and did nothing to free herself. It felt warm, safe, and inviting. Zuli had hugged a few young men before; they had become good friends and wanted more than friendship, but she never allowed it to go beyond this point. Besides, she never felt comfort in their embraces, as she did in

Lamar's.

"Thank you for catching me, Lamar, but you can let go of me now," Zuli whispered. Lamar took his time since he enjoyed holding his love close, her feet dangling in midair.

"Yes, of course," he replied with reluctance. But instead, he recited an eloquent Rumi quote to Zuli: "'Days that are gone, say go, it matters not – you stay, none are purer than you.'" Regretfully, he let her go as she blushed like a spring rose.

Zuli and Lamar were greeted by an altogether colorless garden. They did not see the usual array of exquisite shades they had grown accustomed to. Lamar looked back at the combination of colors on the carriage and Mr. Matek. Now, he saw the same combination in the garden: black and white.

"How odd is this place?" Zuli questioned.

They stood on black ground while the sky overhead was stark white. The garden was shaped in a perfect circle. In the outermost part of the circle were enormous black trees. The rest of the space was covered by endless beds of snow white roses.

"Odd, indeed," replied Lamar, Zuli standing by his side, peering into the Garden of Roses. Just as they were going to look around, they heard someone say, "*Vous êtes arrivés, magnifique. Bienvenue!*" ("Wonderful, you have arrived. Welcome!") Zuli and Lamar were startled and turned to see who spoke to them in French. Frantic, they searched everywhere, but did not see anyone.

"*Bonjour, mes amis* (hello, my friends). I am over

here, please do turn around." Zuli and Lamar turned around on demand in a clockwise rotation. What they saw was astonishing, to say the least. Perched on Mr. Matek's back was a striking parrot. The parrot winked, then did a Zuli-like curtsy by flaring a glorious white wing into the air. As usual, Lamar did a bow with his right hand on his chest, while Zuli felt pride in her methodical curtsy. "I received a message from Kasib in the Garden of Lily Ponds that you were on your way with our good friend, Mr. Matek.

"I welcome you to the Garden of Roses, where your last challenges await; of course, one of which is the overall search for the unseen fig blossom. At the precise moment you complete your trials, when the time is ripe, your journey shall come to an end. The oncoming path will take you back to the Garden of Ali Mardan, where Adir eagerly awaits your return."

Zuli and Lamar were fascinated by the bird's beauty. They had seen parrots who could speak a few words before, but none like this particular one, who was fluent, switching back and forth between languages. Zuli did not speak French, but Lamar could understand the brilliant bird comfortably resting on Mr. Matek's back, which resembled polished onyx.

Her supple feathers looked sheerer than deemed possible. The parrot had a curved, strong beak which appeared to be made of quartz, opal, and moonstone all compressed together. They were fascinated by the bird's unique beauty. Each feather was delicately manicured and laid atop one another. Her eyes were black, yet they were softened by exaggerated, curled lashes. As if she was not stunning enough, she also had a crown of feathers atop her small head. Her crest was a burst of tall, black feathers. The feathers seemed as though they were trimmed by a razor-sharp pair of scissors in the hands of a talented hair stylist. The parrot was truly a whimsical creature.

Lamar was rather confused. The exotic bird looked oddly familiar to him.

"*Pardonnez-moi* (excuse me), I suppose introductions are in order. My name is Tueti. I have traveled from the Garden of Doves to assist you. Before I explain the challenges, please let me know if you have any questions. I am willing to answer any inquiries you may have at this time. The baffled looks on your faces indicate that you may have a list of issues."

Lamar asked the one question that Zuli had in mind. "You mentioned that you have come from the Garden of Doves. Did the score of doves who helped Mr. Matek over the chasm come with you, Madam Tueti?"

"*Oui* (yes), the doves journeyed with me, and they shall return with me at the time of my departure. Please address me as Tueti, *merci* (thank you)."

Lamar confidently replied, "*D'accord, avec plaisir* (Okay, with pleasure)."

Zuli smiled at Lamar with pride for sounding so French. She made a mental note that, once she returned to the palace, she would begin learning French. Although she was fluent in English and had considered learning Italian, she was prepared to accept the task of learning French so that she and Lamar could converse in four different languages. His English was not as fluent as hers, but he was still learning. They both spoke Dari, also known as Farsi, one of the official languages of Afghanistan. Of course, the other official language, which they had to learn in school, was Pashto. In addition, they could read Arabic, but that harbored some difficulties since they could only understand certain words and short phrases. However, later on, Zuli learned that Lamar also spoke fluent Hindi. He told her he learned to speak Hindi by watching Indian movies. She decided to ask him to teach her some words in French during the remainder of their journey.

Later, Lamar and Zuli rested in the carriage and discussed everything Tueti shared. Tomorrow morning, they were to set off to meet Tueti's lifelong friend. Her friend was in dire need of help, but Tueti did not give any more specifics except that, in the morning, they would travel east to where her friend waited.

During their casual conversation, a light bulb switched on in Lamar's mind. "Oh wow!" he exclaimed, looking at Zuli in disbelief. Zuli noticed the look of utter shock on Lamar's face and demanded to know what was wrong. "Nothing is wrong, don't be alarmed Zuli. It just occurred to me why Tueti looked so familiar. I had a nagging feeling I had seen her before. She is identical to a parrot I once drew on a wall in our home."

Zuli remarked, half in earnest and half in jest, "Well, you sound a bit crazy. What would a drawing on the wall have to do with Tueti?"

"I don't know, but I intend to find out tomorrow when we see her," he declared. "She looks just like my drawing. I was nine-years-old when my parents bought a new home. It was a large open space, and had tall white walls. The day we moved in, you could still smell the fresh paint. As you know, I adore art, and I like to think of myself as a fairly good artist."

"One particular wall attracted my attention: the wall in the entrance hall. It was quite spacious and everyone had to enter through this foyer. It looked like a painter's canvas, ready for the touch of a brush stroke, a splatter of color, and the opportunity to capture the mind's image for the joy of onlookers.

"The image flying around my creative psyche that day was a parrot. It was a special gift from me to my parents."

Lamar had to stop talking for a second because Zuli was laughing, knowing where the story led. Lamar could not help laughing, too, since Zuli's laugh was so contagious.

Between giggles, he continued, "I knew that, when my parents came home, they would be overjoyed and reward me for bringing life and character to that wall. Well, Zuli, I worked hard to make sure no details were missed. I wanted the parrot to look like none other, with an exotic serene face. I had a black colored pencil, which I used to give this soulful parrot a majestic crown of feathers. I waited late into the evening to surprise my parents. Surely, my artistic creation was bound to incite cheers. As you can guess, there were no cheers, unless you count the few shrills of horror that left my mother as my father comforted her."

With a chuckle, Lamar added, "I did, however, catch a glimpse of my father's bemused look and a hint of a smile looking at the parrot, then back at me. He reassured my mother and guided her away from where I stood, immobilized by her shrill yelps. Yes, I was reprimanded; however, I must say that I am still grateful to my father for saving me from a well-deserved punishment. While my mother disapproved, my father loved the drawing and ensured it remained untouched. Over time, my mother grew accustomed to being greeted by the parrot day in and day out, no matter which way she went in the house."

Zuli chimed in, "Are you going to ask Tueti about it tomorrow? What if she thinks we're *both* a bit mad? I don't want her to think that about *me*."

"I will make sure she doesn't think that about you. Over time, though, I'm sure that you will have no trouble proving that all by yourself." They laughed jovially, now familiar with one another's sense of humor, vital to their growing friendship. Zuli's upbringing was serious; rules were always imposed. This caused her to have a stoic and responsible nature. However, what she most valued in herself was her witty sense of humor. She had always expected her future life partner to possess similar characteristics, but above all, he should be able to make her laugh with his wit. She realized that the young man sitting next to her possessed all of the traits she wanted in a partner. Lamar was above and beyond her expectations – fit to be a prince, if not a king.

Lamar continued, "You see, Zuli, when the time came to sell the house, it sold without delay because the first buyer loved the drawing of the parrot on the wall. Just so you know, the parrot became a source of comfort for me. It felt as though I had a friend who was always there to greet me. Whenever I walked by, I made sure to smile at the parrot."

Zuli added, "Well, did you know that many cultures around the world admire parrots as a symbol of positive energy and good luck? Some view parrots as divine birds symbolizing freedom."

"In fact, I did not know that, Zuli, but I had a feeling you would know about parrots, just like you knew about the moods of fish," Lamar joked.

They teased one another for a while about who had more knowledge of birds, fish, insects, and more. Lamar sensed Zuli was more at ease with him, which encouraged him to open up to her. Not knowing how she felt about the love letter, though, was beyond unnerving and sometimes he wished he had never written it. What if she thought him a buffoon, a clown, a chump? *Well*, he thought to himself, *it was too late now*. There was no regret or shame in confessing one's love. Even if Zuli thought him a fool, it would not alter his feelings for her. He may have been nervous, but more than that, he was proud of himself. It took a man of strong beliefs and an enlightened soul to acknowledge the sounds of his own heart. His heart loved Zuli. If he had to do it all over again, he would write an even longer and more profound love letter. He would tell the entire world, because true love was the only seed that bred beauty within its roots, deeply planted like the lotus flower's roots in the Garden of Lily Ponds. Those roots remained intact for an endless time.

As the day came to an end, Zuli watched Lamar lay down for a few hours' rest. She stood up and moved away from the carriage to take a better look at the garden. She took out her notebook and began to draw the moon and surrounding areas. The moon was overwhelming and loomed down upon them. Earlier in the evening, the cusp of the moon sat so close to the horizon that they had the urge to reach out to see if they could touch it. The moon seemed larger than the entire garden in its full, bright glory. In its presence, Zuli felt tiny and humbled. The moonlight gleamed down like scattered diamonds twinkling in all directions. Its glistening glitter reflected off the white rose beds and bordering black trees. It covered the dark ground like tidal waves of silver water beneath her feet.

She looked back at Lamar, wishing she could share this moment with him, but he was fast asleep. Zuli continued to draw in her notebook, and then turned the page to Lamar's love letter. She began to read it again. Reading each word with intent, she wished she was back in the lily ponds. She recalled writing underwater in the pond. It was the most rare and exceptional experience of her life. Now she was in a different place, sitting with the moon. She knew it was time to explore her feelings for Lamar and felt obliged to answer his letter. To her surprise, exploring her feelings did not take much time, as her heart leapt out of her chest, landing at her feet. She was struck between her heartbeats; she realized she was truly in love. This surge of feeling was unlike anything she had experienced.

Why on earth am I crying? she thought. *I must be going soft, or maybe I'm too tired.* Even so, her tears felt pleasantly unfamiliar, and she turned to a blank page in her notebook, musing for a long while. Lamar had no idea that she, too, was a lover of poetry. He did not know that words moved her to different stages of thought-provoking interpretations, deep awareness, and insightful knowing. Her family enjoyed poetry. As a result, she too enjoyed literature and creative writing. She wished now that she had spent more time memorizing poems because she could not think of one verse appropriate for the feelings rampaging through her, filling her heart with love. Love for Lamar.

The Love Letter

Dearest Lamar,

Long ago, I saw a painting of a fairyland in a book where the bright moon loomed in the center of the darkest space. It made the blackness of the land a velvet obscurity. Tonight, I have found myself in that fairyland, under the bright gaze of a clear full moon. It is as though I can see myself as one sees in a mirror. More than reflecting my essence, the pure face of the moon captures even the black strands of my hair blown in all directions. Of all the places and spaces in this vast universe, I am caught and found in-between the life and love of this wonderland, far from our realities.

The love between us is separated by many paces, but your letter was all I needed to close the gap between our souls. You have told me that you're my soulmate and a protector of mine. You have roamed the streets of Kabul just far enough behind me to remain unseen, yet close enough to make sure I was protected. You waited patiently through the years for that magical moment when your hand reached for mine and pulled me into a mysterious oasis, through the mystical fig tree standing in the Garden of Ali Mardan.

I want you to know that, as you sleep under the charming gaze of the moon, I write this letter in response to yours. Perhaps I will be the future queen of the land we love. However, I shall never view you as a humble citizen at my service. Never! Tonight, I read, recited, and deciphered each word written in your neat handwriting. Each and every word bounced off the surface of my heart just to come back and sink deeply in captivation. Your printed words murmured jingles of love and awakened an old, familiar feeling in the seat of my heart. It was dormant, but now it blazes through these chambers. I have seen your esteemed glances follow me with admiration. All the while, I, too, have observed you, and have been fulfilled by our effortless connection. Above all, I have known from the very beginning that you would never betray nor hurt me. Now, I see how the grand words of Hafiz ring true as, "Your heart and my heart are very, very old friends," and it was fate that brought me to you. It was meant to be exactly as it is. How delightful that our hearts echo the same sounds of love. I am thankful that we were chosen to find the unseen fig blossom and bring the happiness we have witnessed on our enchanted journey of gardens upon gardens to our homeland.

I will place my letter of love in the inner left pocket of your jacket, close to your heart. I wish you were awake to sit with me under the moon's strikingly exalted presence. You, too, would feel its fanciful forces casting a mighty spell. "The moon stays bright when it doesn't avoid the night"— I'm positive you know this quote by Rumi. Regardless of the bleakness of our nation and its populace, we shall persevere. I remain hopeful and look forward to a bright future. Yes, I shall cherish the memories of our dreamlike journey within the layers of my heart. Most of all, nothing will ever separate us. We shall remain connected by fate and design, through all realms.

Yours,
Zuli

The next morning, Lamar's gaze met a bleached white sky overhead. He was yet to see the sun in this colorless garden, which was lined with black trees on the outskirts of a circular ring of white roses. He stood on his seat in the carriage and looked into the surroundings, but Zuli was not in sight.

He disembarked the vessel onto the black ground and approached Mr. Matek. He patted the horse, lovingly caressing its white mane. Lamar was close to Mr. Matek's face; he looked into the horse's astonishing brown eyes, filled with marvel and wonder. "Mr. Matek, have you seen Zuli?" He nodded his head, motioning to the garden's right side. Lamar patted him with adoration and walked towards the right end of the circular garden. He searched for Zuli, the black haired and petite framed princess who stole his heart long before he even knew he had one.

Lamar passed countless beds of white roses. The roses filled the air with an unmistakable, delicate scent. It was the tantalizing fragrance only a rose could produce to seduce. It reminded Lamar of the strong, yet sweet, aroma of rose water. Immediately, it jogged his memory; he thought of the cool drink his mother used to make with rose water, called *aab-e-rayhaan*. It was a simple drink of pure ice-water mixed with infused rose water, sugar, and black seeds, known as chia or mountain basil seeds. After being soaked in the water, they burst into a multitude of fuzzy gray seeds. Lamar recalled how the infused rose water tickled his nose and woke his senses with a mere whiff. It was the only drink that entirely quenched his thirst during the hot summer months.

Further into the rose garden, Lamar spotted the one for whom he searched. There she was, right where she should be, reading her notebook under a tree. He walked towards her and, as he got closer, Lamar noticed Tueti was next to Zuli, but she was more focused on the black tree under which they sat. Watching Zuli hold her notebook in one hand and turn the page with the other, Lamar remembered sitting under a tree in the garden of their home, waiting for his father to read him a storybook. His father also held books in that manner, using his right hand to turn the pages neatly, as though each was more precious than a gilded leaflet. His father took pleasure in reading children's stories to Lamar, explaining or translating as needed. He did so to make sure Lamar grasped the true themes of the stories, filling pages upon pages of typed black letters. During winter nights, the same ritual continued inside the house, when they read around the wood-burning heater. Time after time, his father stopped reading just to throw a few logs into the heater to keep the sitting room warm and cozy. The reminiscences of those priceless times were imprinted upon Lamar's mind. They were invaluable gifts from his father, who always left Lamar's creative mind immensely inspired with delightful entertainment. Hence, Lamar's creativity and inventive rule-breaking got him in some sticky situations over the years.

Lamar's attention came back to the trees where Zuli sat. He noticed how very dark and uninviting the entire surroundings were. There was something strange about those grand trees that disturbed him to his core. He could not, however, pinpoint what it was that troubled his aura. He noticed Tueti seemed distraught and paced back and forth, glancing upwards every few seconds.

Tueti saw Lamar approaching and called out, "*Bonjour, Monsieur Lamar* (good morning, Mr. Lamar)." For the next hour, Tueti explained the story of the challenges ahead and the situation of the Garden of Roses. Upon her request, Lamar removed the magical branch with the silver tip from the left inner pocket of his jacket. Reaching for the branch, he felt something else. He pulled it out halfway and realized it was a few notebook pages skillfully folded to fit inside his pocket. Lamar's heart leapt out of his chest. The pages looked like those in Zuli's notebook. Right away, he knew it was a letter from Zuli.

Tueti looked at him and said, "Lamar, are you feeling okay? You look as though you have seen a ghost."

"No. Yes. I mean, I'm okay. I was just thinking about the trees and wondering why they're all black. It gives me a chilling feeling," he responded.

"Oh, yes, I understand your concern. You are indeed a wise young man to have sensed the dark energy of this place."

Zuli looked at Lamar with curiosity, as he fidgeted with his pocket for a few quick seconds. Zuli's face turned bright red; she knew he had found her letter and tried to shove it back in his pocket.

Seeing him struggle brought a smile to her face that she did not want Lamar to see, so she quickly got up and said, "Yes, Tueti, I also sensed an aura of melancholy in these trees. I felt like they called me closer, as though my presence gave them comfort. Do you think

I am wrong to feel this way?"

Tueti replied, *"Pas du tout* (not at all). As a matter of fact, you're observant. Your connection to these ancient, longstanding trees is why you can feel the gloom in their hearts. They have survived invasions and the forays of scores of cruel creatures that have roamed our worlds for quite some time. Throughout the centuries, the trees have remained – enduring many trials and great suffering. Ever since their original lush green pigment changed to black, they are no longer hale and hearty, nor do they produce fruit." Once again, Lamar skeptically peered around, then walked up to Tueti and took a deliberate look at her features.

Before he could even think, the words flew out of him. "Tueti, you may think that I have lost my mind, but I think I have seen you before. You look very much like…"

Zuli cut him off, laughing nervously, and added, "Oh, Tueti, Lamar claims that you are the same parrot he once drew on the wall of his home back in Kabul. Please do tell him that his imagination has taken a leap beyond reality."

Tueti looked from the giggling face of Zuli to Lamar's somewhat embarrassed one. "Well," said Tueti, "How can I explain this delicately? Zuli, how did you feel when you first saw Mr. Matek in the Garden of Lily Ponds; do you recall at all?"

As soon as Lamar heard her question, his expression changed. He smiled, turned to Zuli, and crowed, "Yes, Zuli, go ahead and tell us how you felt when you first saw Mr. Matek. If you don't remember, I could recount the entire episode for Tueti." Zuli was caught off guard, looking between Lamar's striking but teasing smile and Tueti's exquisite features.

Zuli awkwardly cleared her throat. "As you well know, Mr. Matek was in my dreams. I didn't draw him on a wall like someone else." Shooting Lamar a look of satisfaction, she turned back to Tueti and awaited her response. Tueti spread her glorious wings and flew away from them, saying they should follow her. She headed to an area filled with white roses far away from the trees.

"Foremost, let me tell you that I was created in the mind of a boy who was only nine years of age. His young mind gave life to me when artistic hands rendered his imagination on the surface of a grand white wall." Zuli gasped and covered her mouth with both hands, looking to Lamar. He bore a stunned expression plastered on his face.

"Are you the same parrot I drew on the wall of our home that summer day?" Lamar spoke in astonishment.

"But of course," answered an overjoyed Tueti. "I am the same parrot, created in the mind of a talented artist with supernatural foresight. However, I am only here to guide you through your challenge."

Tueti's expression darkened. "I have been in this exclusively black and white garden because I was created so. My usual habitat is the Garden of Iridescence, where my parrot family awaits my long-overdue return. I do not belong here with the doves and roses. Unless I fulfill my duties today, I may never find my way home. I have awaited your arrival for all these years."

Lamar could not stop himself from moving closer and kneeling on the ground in front of Tueti. He placed his hands on her sides in a tender manner. His voice was husky and filled with raw emotion when he said, "May I have the honor of hugging you, Madam Tueti, my sacred friend?" Without waiting for her response, Lamar picked her up, brought her close to his heart, and hugged her dearly. In that moment, Lamar found himself standing in front of the great white wall in his parents' home. It was the home where he was loved the most, and where he felt safest. He could smell the remnants of his mother's cooking and hear footsteps coming from the outside. In his mind's eye, he saw the front door open and his parents enter; he stood proudly by his drawing of a parrot.

He heard his own voice announce with cheer, "Look, look! I did this! I drew this! This is a gift for you, *Madar* (mother). Do you like it, do you?" He remembered the happy days he spent with his family in their home. He remembered his father reading to him.

But then, he clearly saw a war zone and everything lost within it. He could hear the sounds of bullets, warplanes, and tanks. He saw his family torn apart. He remembered the death of his little sister and the mournful wailing of his parents. Zuli jolted him from his thoughts by putting her hand on his shoulder.

Lamar did not realize that he was still hugging Tueti and his face was drenched with tears of pain. He longed for his family and to be back within the walls of his home. He relived his short yet entire life when he held Tueti against his heart.

Lamar looked at Tueti against his chest and mustered an apology, "I am terribly sorry, Madam! I do apologize. I don't know what came over me." He put her down. When he stood, Zuli put her arms around Lamar and hugged him like he had never been hugged before. After so many years of loneliness, it was the first time he felt an absolute sense of comfort and belonging. He wrapped his arms around Zuli and pulled her closer. They hugged until Lamar's tears subsided and he was able to release her.

Per Tueti's instructions, they set off towards a particular field of white roses. Tueti was perched on Lamar's shoulder. It suited her well since his height allowed her to see ahead far into the distance. She moved from time to time between his right shoulder and outstretched left forearm. She sat on Lamar's strong arm to be closer to Zuli when she wanted to chat. Since the specific field of white roses was not far, they preferred to walk. Meanwhile, Mr. Matek was a few paces behind, his elegant vessel in tow. On the way, Tueti told them they would use the second enchantment to free her confidant, and best friend, the mother dove. Zuli asked if the mother dove had a name.

"Oui (yes)," she replied, "her name is Sadaf. All the doves and parrots call her Sadaf the Mother Dove. Her name translates to mother-of-pearl and her impact on this garden is just as rare and valuable. She is positively pure, as her name would suggest." Zuli adored the name; it was simple, yet it rang with a flare of sophistication.

Lamar agreed with Zuli. "That's exactly how your

name sounds to my ears, Zuli." Upon hearing his kind words, Zuli gave Lamar a hint of a smile and reached her right hand out towards him. Without missing a beat, he took her hand in his. After all they had shared throughout their journey, it was the first time they walked through a garden holding hands.

Lamar was ready to use the silver-tipped tree branch. There were two more wishes. At that point, he was not yet sure what the last wish was for, but Tueti assured them they would know in good time. Lamar felt her rise in the air from atop his shoulder. She looked down at them and announced they had arrived. They had reached a point where Zuli and Lamar should have been able to see the mother dove. They were puzzled and looked to Tueti for clarification. All they could see was another field of white roses, but in a different shape than the others.

Tueti's chipper demeanor changed. She sighed, "Here lies a most compassionate bird, one who has remained regal and poised despite her inability to soar." Zuli and Lamar were still puzzled, but did not dare interrupt her. They were baffled; they did not see the mother dove anywhere. They continued to listen, holding hands and standing shoulder to shoulder.

Tueti went on to say, "Sadaf and I are lifelong friends. She is a guardian and a defender of *haque* (justice). She has an innate, soft nature. She is devoted, charitable, and has a keen perception, making her more sympathetic and wiser than any that I have known."

Zuli and Lamar spoke in unison: "Where is Sadaf? Can we not see her? Is she hidden in one of the trees?"

Tueti smiled. "My, you two do think alike. To answer

your questions, Sadaf is not in the trees. She is right in front of us on the ground. She has been shackled by the vicious crows that control this garden."

Zuli and Lamar peered over Tueti and her outstretched wings. "All we see is a vast spread of roses, Tueti."

"No, my friends, those aren't just roses." Suddenly, they could make out Sadaf's shape. The mother dove was held down by thick black wires overtop her legs and the tips of her delicate wings. Her white feathers were camouflaged within the bed of roses. She was immobile to the point of visible discomfort, and the harrowing scene was traumatizing to both Lamar and Zuli. Observing the incredulous looks on their faces, Tueti continued.

"The evil crows made Sadaf their prisoner instead of taking all her dove hatchlings. These crows are of a wretched and dejected nature. Their survival is based on relishing and savoring the despair of their surroundings. Hence, all of these centuries-old, once green trees lack color, serve no purpose, bear no fruit, and exhibit no beauty.

"Sadaf sacrificed her freedom for the liberty of her entire family, who await her return to the Garden of Doves. Once our second enchantment is cast, Sadaf the Mother Dove will rise into the skies, free at last. The inhabitants of both grounds hope her release will breathe life back into every living thing in the two gardens. This phenomenon can only happen when a heart is filled to the brim with love, even in the face of such cruelty. You two must remember this for your journey. When you are faced with harsh cruelty, the only means of survival are to drown your soul in the sea of compassion and drench your wounds in the depths of a forgiving and merciful well. Only then will your spirit remain strong and resilient. No degree of hardship can fragment a spirit of steel."

Lamar and Zuli still held hands while listening to Tueti's profound dialogue. They wished they could write down all that she articulated. Zuli knew that, in her twelve years of education, she had not learned as much as she had on her journey, and just now through Tueti's wise words.

Based on Tueti's instructions, the three stood in a specific area of the garden. Tueti faced her two young friends. "Are you pointing the enchanted tree branch to the west, Lamar?"

"Yes, Tueti, it is pointing west."

"As soon as we utter the very last word, take cover. The magnitude of the events that will unfold may be overwhelming. Do you understand?"

"Yes, we understand," chimed the adventurers.

"Very well. Now, both of you repeat after me. The second enchantment is: *O' free the mother bird held captive far too long. Let her elongate her great wings and sing her sweet songs. No worldly evil is without its good times. Choose the righteous path through this rhyme.*"

When the last word was spoken, Tueti flew to Lamar's shoulder and shouted, "Step back! Step back!"

Lamar pulled Zuli back further into the fields. Sure enough, the ground started to move. It felt like an earthquake to him. However, it was no ordinary quake, and reminded him of the terrifying earthquakes he experienced as a child in Kabul. He felt it was the most startling experience nature had ever taken him through. Lamar drew Zuli closer and shielded her and Tueti with his body while the white roses gradually rose in the air. To Lamar, it was like an airplane taking off from a runway and launching straight into the atmosphere. The sound was as deafening as a volcano eruption. Zuli covered her ears. Lamar's vision was blurred by heaps of *khaak* (dust) rising into the air. Various pieces of unfamiliar flurry sprayed from overhead.

As the dust subsided, they witnessed a splendid scene. Sadaf the Mother Dove now hovered above them, leaving behind her imprint where the smallest, white rosebuds sprouted. At that moment, Tueti stretched her wings and took off skyward, lingering at a reasonable altitude. As they looked up, Lamar and Zuli were awestruck by Sadaf. She was a brilliant white dove with vast, elegant wings covered in the softest feathers. They resembled a sea of pearls, like Mr. Matek's carriage. She flapped her wings, gliding ever so gently and looking at the line of trees behind Zuli and Lamar. She swooped closer to the ground at an unbelievable speed. She went to the far side of the garden and began to fly very low over the black trees. At that point, Zuli and Lamar had to cover their eyes because debris was flying all around. Lamar reached out and snatched some right out of the air.

"What are these things, Lamar? Can you tell?"

"They are black feathers, Zuli. I believe they're the feathers of the cruel crows. I'm not sure what Sadaf is doing, but I can see these feathers coming off the trees near her. I don't even see Tueti around. Do you?"

Zuli squinted, shielding her eyes from the feathers and dust. Both the air and the entire Garden of Roses were filled with nothing but black feathers. In the distance, Zuli saw Sadaf flying over every single tree.

"Yes, yes, I see Tueti! Lamar, look this way!" They watched her land on each tree after Sadaf flew over it.

All the black trees seemed a bit taller. They could see that, in reality, the tree trunks and branches were never pigmented black. It appeared as though millions of crows were nestled, making the trees look so murky and bleak. The crows now flew away since their captive was free. After all, the enchantment said *no worldly evil is without its good times*. The crows disappeared and the trees began to shed the black feathers.

As they witnessed the magic, Lamar and Zuli walked towards the wooded area. The closer they drew, the more implausible it became. They saw scores and scores of baby doves fly from the trees and take to the air.

"Lamar, this is unbelievable. Sadaf remained captive because of these doves." Zuli recalled a writing from her notebook: *The greatest givers relinquish all glory when, with a full heart, they give solely of themselves*. Zuli had eagerly shared her writing with her mother, and she was told that she would one day be an inspiring messenger of peace.

As they drew closer to the trees, Zuli and Lamar gasped.

"Wow! These are all fig trees!" The trees were covered in opulent green leaves. The entire garden was filled with white doves, and they all circled the mother dove, Sadaf. The black feathers turned to dust covering the black ground, and the sky overhead hinted at rays of sunshine peeking through the white clouds. When the last tree was freed from its burden of captivity, Sadaf and Tueti turned in midair and flew towards the two spectators. By then, all the feathers had vanished into the depths of the dirt. The Garden of Roses was brilliantly white, encircled by ancient fig trees much bigger than their tree in the Garden of Ali Mardan.

Wide-eyed, they watched Sadaf's fluid descent. Tueti flew close by; she looked like a baby dove compared to the massiveness of Sadaf. They landed adjacent to where Zuli and Lamar stood. Sadaf's greeting was warm and welcoming. Zuli and Lamar greeted her with words of adoration, and then asked for permission to approach. She spoke in a mellow and delicate tone. She had a graceful appearance, yet her entire body was made of powerful muscles, which enabled her strength and speed. Sadaf had the face of a charming ballerina: large hazel eyes, long brown eyelashes, and a pinkish beak. The rest of the mother dove's figure was covered in a white layering of perfect feathers woven together. She smiled warmly at them before turning to Tueti with a look of fondness.

"Oh, my dearest Tueti, how can I ever thank you for your support throughout these years? You came and went, always keeping an eye on my baby doves and me. Even more so, you guided our young friends' steps to where I laid captive."

Sadaf beamed. "Oh, just look! Look around at this garden and the fig trees now lush and alive once again! As you take flight with the scores of baby doves, I bid you *bon voyage* (good journey). The doves will travel with you only to the Garden of Doves; from there, you will continue on to your true home, the Garden of Iridescence, where your entire family is eagerly waiting."

Once again, the goodbyes were heart-wrenching. However, what Lamar did not expect was for Tueti to spread her wings to their fullest extent and wrap him in a hug. Who would have thought that parrots could cry? Tueti not only shed tears, but also thanked Lamar for creating her. Zuli could see that Lamar was overwhelmed and, for once, at a loss for words.

"Remember these words *mes amis* (my friends): when your inner mirror is kept spotless, the light will know where to reflect best. You are the light and delight of all those connected to you. Reflect and remain resolute during trying times to enlighten your community."

As the dove family prepared for their departure, Sadaf told Lamar and Zuli she would be back in no time after seeing her family off. Zuli suggested to Lamar that they examine the fig trees closely.

"Let's go! That's the best idea I've heard all day," Lamar said, pulling Zuli in that direction.

"Why are you running so fast, Lamar? Stop, will you?" But Lamar did not feel like stopping. In fact, he just kept going.

"I'll race you! I bet you can't beat me in running like you did in swimming!"

Zuli freed her hand from his grip and sprinted past him. "That's cheating, you know!"

Before Zuli knew it, Lamar caught up to her. He was about to pass when she grabbed the back of his jacket. Zuli held on for dear life and pulled him back, all while trying to pass him. They both started to pull one another back to get ahead. The race petered out since they were overtaken by laughter, wrestling to see who could win.

They reached the fig trees. Zuli went up to one tree and hugged it with open arms. In the heart of the Garden of Roses, Lamar watched the love of his life do exactly what she had done since she was about six-years-old in the Garden of Ali Mardan. He was anxious to find some alone time to read the letter still neatly tucked into his left pocket. Lamar moved closer to where Zuli stood. She was now observing the branches and leaves. Whatever came over Lamar was beyond him, because he took her hand. As soon as she turned around, he stepped in.

"I hope you can forgive me, my princess." Before she could question him, he brought her hands up. While holding her gaze, he kissed her left hand first, then her right. He bent towards her, softly kissed her forehead, and then their lips locked in one tender kiss. He kissed Zuli under the fig tree.

The kiss was from the depths of Lamar's soul, with a heart full of absolute and resolute love for Zuli. She was the one his soul knew from long ago. Zuli, for the entirety of an eternity, would always be his. This much he knew all too well.

Chapter 6

The Homeward Journey

> "Wherever you go – east, west, north, or south –
> think of it as a journey into yourself.
> The one who travels into itself travels the world."
>
> ~ Shams Tabriz

Zuli and Lamar sat with arms entwined, holding one another for dear life. They held their breaths and hoped for the best. They were not given even an opportunity to think. Before they knew it, they had boarded the coziest seating they had yet experienced. Sadaf the Mother Dove informed them that she was designated to take them home, and they would leave on schedule, not a second later.

Lamar recalled Tueti's words: "When the time is ripe, your journey shall then come to an end. The oncoming path will take you back." Now they were homeward bound, west all the way until they reached the Garden of Ali Mardan. Adir, of course, told them in the beginning that their journey was designed to enhance their mindfulness. There were lessons within lessons the pair needed to learn. Those lessons would steer them towards finding the true essence of the fig blossom, and the foundation for everlasting unity.

Lamar's thoughts returned to Sadaf as she spoke of Adir. "Our mutual wise friend, Adir, awaits. Be mindful that the set time of our arrival is Friday at high noon." Friday was considered a day of relaxation and bliss. "Should we arrive even a minute late, Adir will turn back into a solid rock. Or rather, he will appear more like an imposing mountain sitting high and mighty, never to utter another word."

"Sadaf, with all due respect, we cannot leave yet. We still haven't fulfilled our main challenge, the search for the fig blossom."

"Absolutely, Sadaf. Lamar has a point," chimed Zuli. "We can't leave just yet. While you left to see the family of doves off, Lamar and I searched for the blossom with diligence, only to end up empty-handed. Lamar even climbed the trees. I told him he shouldn't, but he assured me you wouldn't mind."

"Yes, he was right, Zuli. I don't mind if you two climb the trees to search, as long as you refrain from damaging even one leaf or breaking a single branch. That would be the ultimate dishonor to nature. I know the two of you would never harm any of the trees. For that matter, I understand you would not harm anything in nature since you both have hearts of nurturers and souls of protectors."

Upon Sadaf's inspiring statement, once again, Zuli could not help but think of the destitute population back home, chopping down trees to be used for warming their homes. Many trees were missing from where they had stood for centuries. Most streets were barren of trees, offering no shade on a hot summer day. Zuli had seen firsthand, however, the importance of keeping nature intact on their journey. Although she had a deep adoration for all life in nature, she was, nonetheless, taken aback by the lessons she learned from observing the gardens' maintenance by those not of her species. Every little leaf was protected in such a way to continue its splendor.

Zuli reflected on the trials they had faced. Each challenge was meant to save the respective garden, from the roots to the center. In return, all the gardens' inhabitants would thrive for countless eras to come. This, she knew, would be one of the fundamental lessons she would share with the public. She already knew that, once the illiterate or misinformed were educated, the outcome would be positive and permanent. She made a note to add these musings to her long list of matters needing implementation upon her return to the palace.

She also noted that she wanted to tell Lamar about her apple tree incident. Although she remembered that day as if it was yesterday, in reality, it was over twelve years ago.

On a hot Thursday afternoon, Zuli's visiting cousins, out of sheer boredom, encouraged her to climb the apple tree that stood in the palace backyard, visible from the room where her grandmother spent her days. That day, her grandmother was away and did not hear or see the commotion. Zuli remembered climbing the tree so quickly that, for a minute, she felt like a superhero. She promised her cousins she would find the biggest apples at the very top to throw down. Those were the juiciest and sweetest. Everyone had their arms up, yelling for an apple to be thrown down, so she did exactly that.

How many apples did I throw down? Zuli now thought to herself. Too many. No one could catch them, so the apples hit the ground, smashing into pieces on contact. After a while, there were no more apples in her reach. The worst part: she was stuck at the very top and could not find sure footing to get down. Her cousins left the apple-covered backyard in fear of being caught by an adult. She was stuck. The culprit was as evident as the countless pieces of splattered apples; thus, she could not even try to blame it on any of her cousins.

A smile crossed Zuli's face as she recalled everyone in the palace coming together under the tree to contrive her safe descent. The gardener brought out several ladders, but they were all too short. Ultimately, the gardener volunteered – or, come to think of it, she was not quite sure if he had volunteered or was forced – to climb the tree to help retrieve her. At some point, after the gardener made sure she had reached a safer area in the tree, due to the many people yelling instructions from below, he lost his footing and dropped out of the tree in the same way that she dropped apples to her cousins. He landed like a sack of flour in the middle of everyone, face down.

Zuli's heart sank; she knew the inevitable degree of scolding had risen to a volcanic level. For just a moment, they had forgotten the culprit was still in the tree. Then, Zuli realized she still held the apple she took a bite from earlier, when her cousins were around. It had been too sweet and fresh to throw away. She looked down at everyone still huddled over the gardener; since no one was watching, she took another quick bite. As luck would have it, or rather lack of luck, somehow the apple was pushed out of her grip. She watched it fall in slow motion, in the direction of where the gardener still laid flat on his face. The apple hit him precisely where it should not have – smack on the back of his head. Many pairs of eyes shot up all at once, aimed at her like daggers. To this day, she did not know how it happened; it must have been all those faces and eyes that caused her to lose her footing, too, and drop out of the tree. She landed right on top of the gardener.

She was sure Lamar would not find her story as bad as the one he told her about dropping an actual sack of flour on the cook from the roof of his house because he thought that it would be funny. Zuli had laughed and hoped the cook was not injured when Lamar dropped the sack as the cook returned from the neighborhood's *naan-waaei* (bakery) holding freshly baked Afghan *naan* (bread) for lunch. The good news was the cook was not hurt; the bad news was there would not be bread for lunch or dinner. To eat anything without serving bread was unheard of in the Afghan culture, since bread was considered the main staple food in Afghanistan due to overall poverty. The worst news was that Lamar was so terrified of his parents' scolding that he refused to come down from there for two days. The same cook had to serve him food and water on the roof. Lamar learned a valuable lesson during those two daunting days. He told Zuli that, by watching the cook bring him food and water, making sure that no harm came to a very young Lamar, sensations of compassion and contrition reverberated deep within his heart. Each time the cook checked up on him, a seed of empathy was sowed within his core. Thus, Lamar did not want to leave his home for a better and safer life abroad. Based on his values, he chose to stay and serve his country, where that seed took root overtime.

After Zuli's apple tree incident, also at a young age, she learned a valuable lesson from her father about nurturing all living things including trees, fruits, and even the ground on which she walked. He took Zuli to his favorite spot where the fig tree stood at the Garden of Ali Mardan. It was then that Zuli made a deep spiritual connection with the tree, always feeling it called her name. Soon after, she became the protector of the apple tree in the backyard, never again allowing her cousins near its abundance.

Zuli and Lamar had been inseparable since they shared a kiss under the fig trees in the Garden of Roses.

"Zuli, could you kindly loosen your grip on my arm a tad, my lovely? I think you've cut off the blood circulation to my entire arm."

Zuli looked down at Lamar's arm and her grip. "Oh, my goodness, have I been holding on too tightly? I do apologize."

"Well, tight enough that I can't feel my fingers," Lamar joked.

"Okay, now you're exaggerating," said Zuli, squeezing his arm even tighter with a smile.

"Seriously, it's not a problem; it's just that it's been over two hours that you've been tense. I think you can relax and rest assured that nothing will happen to us. We're safe here."

Lamar reassured Zuli, "Besides, I trust Sadaf and know that she wouldn't do anything to put us in harm's way."

"Yes, of course, I believe Sadaf, too, but I told you

that I have a fear of heights. I have had this problem from childhood. My acrophobia was one of the main reasons I fell out of the apple tree, and it has only gotten worse. Though I don't ever let it control me, I wasn't expecting *this*."

As she spoke, Zuli's grip grew even tighter on Lamar's arm. He loved every minute of it, but, being flesh and blood, it *did* start to hurt after a few hours. Holding Lamar, Zuli barely moved; instead, she stretched her neck and glanced below. She looked away and acknowledged the beauty of the scenery far, far beneath them. Lamar leaned to his right to check down below.

Their current situation was an undeniable miracle in its own virtue. Who would have thought they would fly? Although it took a lot of persuasion and encouragement for Sadaf to convince Zuli, Lamar required no convincing. In no time, he had hopped onto Sadaf's plush back, amid soft feathers and massive white wings, for the flight of his life through the clouds and stars, under the moon and sun. In the distance, he could see the grand sun dipping below the horizon's vanishing point, devoted to reappearing within mere hours. He had never seen such a glorious array of inflamed orange and saffron douse the entire world.

For the whole flight, Lamar examined Sadaf's wings and feathers. There was nothing he knew that could compare to them. Even the delicate lace wrapped around the magical silver-tipped tree branch paled next to the richness of each feather, laid upon one another by the hands of nature. Although Sadaf's wings were luxurious, they were still powerful. Lamar thought how one cannot judge anything by its looks. It appeared as if Sadaf was merely a bird of delicate elegance. Yes, it was true she exuded utmost grace, but at the same time, her inner strength resonated with Lamar. This caused him to respect her above all he had encountered thus far as he thought back to the beginning of the flight.

When Sadaf, the caring mother dove, allowed these two passengers on her back, she took off from the grounds of the Garden of Roses. It was another extraordinary experience that neither Lamar nor Zuli would ever forget.

When they took their places on Sadaf's back, she shouted, "Hold on tight, but not too tight! I have you protected within my wings as I carry you on my back, never too far away from my heart, where I hold you near and dear."

"Oh my goodness, how beautiful her words are!" Zuli exclaimed, tightly holding Lamar.

Lamar shouted back to Sadaf, "Please forgive us if we are too heavy. It's all Zuli's fault; I have nothing to do with it."

Sadaf let out a heartfelt laugh and said, "You are not a burden upon my wings, but rather a source of comfort since I cherish your companionship. Have you two not heard the famous saying? Let me see, how does it go?"

Lamar saw that, as Sadaf gathered her thoughts, she also began leaving the ground.

"Yes, yes, I remember: Heavy burdens are carried

within our hearts and upon our wings. Just fly, fly to where love is the lone star, its light knowing no boundaries."

Zuli was listening, but she was also busy trying to deal with her personal fear of heights. On the other hand, Lamar took it all in; their surroundings were spectacular. When Sadaf took off from the garden, her speed, momentum, and thrust caused airborne particles of white pigments to rise up. At first, Lamar thought they were dove feathers. Once again, Lamar was quick; he snatched one from the air as it shot past.

It was a perfect white rose. Lamar wanted to show it to Zuli, but her eyes were half closed. He hid the white rose by his side so she would not see it. While Sadaf ascended into the cosmos, Lamar asked Zuli to observe their surroundings. Rose petals filled the entire garden, all the way up to where Sadaf flew, circling and dancing in unison. At the sight of such a dreamlike image, even Zuli forgot her fears for a moment and sat on her knees to see. As they flew further west, the sea of white petals still covered the entire garden and sky like a sheer white veil, sending Sadaf on her destined journey.

As he watched the unfolding of the Garden of Roses' new beginning, Lamar's senses were beyond fulfilled by the roses' perfume. Although the flowers were crushed by despair, they rose higher than before, dowsing all directions with a fragrance of hope.

Zuli turned to Lamar, awestruck, and said, "I can even smell the elusive fragrance of the roses up here. Can you smell the roses, Lamar?"

"Yes, I can, my dear Zuli." He then presented her with the single white rose he snatched from the air just for her.

He held it out and said, "When the rose opened its heart, it became the mirror of your face. This flower reflects your elegance and loveliness. Do you know, Zuli, that in my eyes, your beauty – especially the purity of your soul – outshines the purity of this rose?"

Not many occasions left Zuli speechless. That moment, however, left her searching for the appropriate words; she did not say a thing. Instead, she took the rose from his outstretched hand to smell the intoxicating perfume. Lamar watched her do so as she had done in the Garden of Lily Ponds, when she gathered the daisies from his fruit platter.

She tucked her hair away from her face and, this time, she placed the flower behind her right ear. "How does that look, Lamar?" she asked timidly.

"The rose is now even rosier," Lamar answered. Zuli giggled, and he reached to hold her closer, giving her an ample sense of security and comfort.

Lamar sensed Zuli beginning to relax. Flying as they did, the wind blew her hair in waves, like how water smoothly bends, winds, and curves around, over, and under rocks.

Lamar took a long look at Zuli covered in the glow of the saffron sunset. He recited Hafiz: *"The earth would die if the sun stopped kissing her."* He then knew he could not possibly love Zuli enough and stored the magic moment in his memory bank.

As the night descended upon them, the ether erupted with blazing stars. Zuli and Lamar held hands, their fingers intertwined. Tiny lights shone in different degrees of glimmering sparks and beams. Admiring the show of lights overhead, Zuli rested in Lamar's embrace in both contentment and exhaustion. Sadaf told them earlier, if they wished, they could lie down as her feathers offered ample warmth and comfort. That night, they both had the best sleep of their lives under the milky skies; it was a canvas coated in the blackest ink, ornamented with each low hanging star, guiding Sadaf on their journey home.

At first, Lamar thought he was dreaming, or that Zuli hummed a very pretty melody. When he opened his eyes, it took him a few seconds to realize that he was still on Sadaf's back, covered in snow white feathers. Across from him, Zuli slept, barely visible, sunk into the feathers' fluff. He realized Sadaf, flying parallel to the ground, hummed an effortless song that the wind carried to him.

Her voice was gentle and soft, yet he could still make out the words: "The one who was in search of oneself found self in you. It was there and then that the journey of the fig blossom took life and came true. As the seekers seek, let's keep hope on its feet. La, la, la, O' no one knows of the coming down and magnitude of blessed heavenly rains. Love is a bird of two wings that flies high above the clouds of all colors... oh, you're awake," Lamar heard Sadaf talking to him.

"Yes, yes, I'm awake now. Did you have a good night and a smooth flight?" Lamar flashed a dashing smile.

Sadaf responded, "I had a lovely flight under the

dazzling galaxy. The brilliant moon shone bright on our westward path, and I had the companionship of the night owls. Look below now, here's a perfect spot for a break."

Sure enough, Sadaf flew low to the ground because she needed a space to land. She descended onto a meadow situated amid fields of yellow sunflowers.

"Oh my," Zuli breathed, now awake. Zuli had once listed her favorite flowers to Lamar, and the sunflower was among them. Sadaf announced that they would rest there for a few hours. She told them that they were getting close to the Garden of Ali Mardan, and checked that Lamar still possessed the magical tree branch. At that point, Sadaf left to visit some friends.

"I wonder who her friends are. Don't you think that we should follow her, Zuli? I'm curious," coaxed Lamar.

"I don't think that's a good idea, Lamar. If she wanted us to go with her, she would've invited us."

"No, I'm going to follow her through these sunflower fields like some sort of thief," jested Lamar.

"Well, I would prefer to take full advantage of this opportunity. We should scour the fields."

"Okay, Zuli, you win, but I'm very good at following others without ever being seen or heard. As you know, I did that with you through the streets of Kabul. You had no idea, and yet, like a shadow that's never farther than arms' reach, I guarded you in and out of the city for years. Even still, because of you, I will pass up this opportunity and not follow Sadaf. Let's explore here then, shall we?"

"Thank you for passing on your *great* idea. Besides, if I had known you were following me, I would have been sneakier," Zuli teased, "I would've used my talents to avert you at every corner just to leave you bewildered and lost."

"*Balai* (yes), of course, you would've done just that to me," Lamar laughed. "I don't doubt you one bit because you're exactly as you said: sneaky, yet sweet as *quand* (cubed sugar)."

Lamar wrapped his arm around Zuli's waist and led her through the fields of sunflowers, guiding her either right or left so she did not trip. Zuli let Lamar guide her in different directions, overjoyed by his presence and completely in love with him. Now, she knew Rumi's words were fitting, as her entire being was beaming: *Love is the soul's light.* She wondered if he had read her letter yet. Of course he had read it! She remembered him fidgeting with the letter in his pocket when he found Tueti and her under the black trees in the Garden of Roses. It was obvious to her, standing in the midst of thousands of acres of sunflower fields, that he loved her to no end. After all, it was designed this way. According to Lamar, his grandfather, plus everyone she had met thus far, knew they were meant to be together as soulmates. Apparently, they knew each other from a past life, or realm.

Zuli was guided sharply to the left by Lamar, who walked behind her with his hands on her waist. Before she realized in which direction he led her, Lamar stopped, turned Zuli around, and said, "With your permission, *azizam* (my dear)." As he did before under the fig trees, he hovered over her for a split second, then proceeded to kiss her in the midst of the sunflower fields. Silently, this kiss murmured sweetness to her heart doing a wild dance. Zuli fell deeper in love. Her soul was brighter than all the stars.

Zuli proclaimed, "Look around! I can't even take in the incredible vastness of these fields. It's just too huge. Do you recall seeing the ocean for the first time?" Before Lamar could answer, Zuli went on, "Really, it's like seeing the ocean for the very first time after being in the desert for a lifetime."

Lamar did not say anything, but he had seen neither ocean nor desert. He also did not want to interrupt Zuli as she expressed herself so eloquently.

"Lamar, try to capture the magic enveloping us. If you capture it now, you shall always keep it within that cage you've described to me, and the magic shall carry you through tough times. We now know that, despite all the suffering we've witnessed in our war-ravaged country, there remain endless possibilities in this world. Those who do not lose hope can always catch it."

He watched her as she stood entranced by the extraordinary beauty around them. Lamar mentally captured the all-encompassing splendor Zuli described. Now more than ever, he knew that the one and only true beauty was the thrilling love rushing through him.

"Doesn't it look as though the sun dropped from the sky and landed on earth's soil just to cover every inch with buttery, yellow rays?" Zuli spoke as if she was in a trance.

Lamar was impressed by Zuli's acute mind. He drew

her closer to him. "My sweet, like you, I am fond of nature. I don't know if I have told you this story once before, but one of my favorite places to visit as a child was my aunt's home. She planted rows and rows of giant sunflowers along the edges of her massive garden. She was famous for her sunflowers that, at times, grew even higher than us! People would come and ask permission to tour the garden.

"Whenever we visited her, I examined the flowers very closely. They were cheerful, yet had an air of hardiness to them. When I was only six, I hid between the flower beds so no one could find me. I had broken off a gigantic sunflower and studied it, bit by bit, for hours. I ended up taking the entire flower apart. The more I took it apart, the more in awe I became at its composition."

Lamar continued, admitting, "I think I even ate parts of the flower and the inner seeds. Soon after, I felt guilty that I had broken the flower, so I took some of its seeds and, with my bare hands, planted them all around the garden. I was certain that they would regrow. Now that I think back, it was such a perfect experience for an inquisitive kid like me."

They stopped walking for a minute. Lamar asked, "Zuli, look at each sunflower. What do you see as a common trait between them?"

Zuli stared and realized that the sunflowers all faced one direction.

"Exactly," Lamar said. "This flower turns its face to the magnificent light of the sun. I have a unique connection and love for the sun, as you have heard me talk about. I believe we should always turn towards the light of the sun and, with open hearts, absorb its warmth to illuminate areas of existing darkness."

"No wonder you were named *Lamar* (sun)," Zuli exclaimed as she reached for his hand and pulled him deeper into the fields. In some places, the flowers were higher than Lamar's six foot frame. The fields swayed as the gentle wind travelled back and forth. They were not sure how far they had gone or from which direction they had come. They were trying to find their way back to meet Sadaf when they both heard it.

From above the imposing sunflowers that tilted as though revealing their contented faces, a distinct sound emerged. As Lamar and Zuli looked up, a fairy-like creature flew by them, then another, and then another, until the entire area swarmed with lightning-fast birds. Lamar squinted against the sun, trying to figure out what the small creatures were.

"Wow! I can't believe we didn't recognize these beauties at first sight, Zuli! Look closely, and you will see that they are incredible hummingbirds! These tiny birds flutter their wings so fast and only appear for a split second before disappearing in a flash of colors."

Zuli raised her arm to coax one to sit on her hand, but they ignored her offer and continued to fly around them. "The hummingbirds are so fast; I can hardly make out their features. All I can see are their rainbow-like feathers," observed Zuli.

"Zuli, I don't know if this is just a coincidence, but whenever I remember my departed loved ones, I am surrounded by hummingbirds, or I see them show up by the window of the shoe repair shop. It could be pure luck, but I was just now thinking about how much my parents and little sister would've enjoyed these sunflower fields."

Zuli chimed in, "As a matter of fact, I know that many cultures see hummingbirds as symbols of joy, especially when they appear out of nowhere."

Lamar smiled at Zuli. "Oh, why am I not surprised that you know this fact. Go on; I am intrigued, my lovely love."

"To the eye, these birds are dainty, yet they are more courageous than we know. They're fearless and determined. They travel long journeys with unwavering resolve and vitality. Lamar, I feel as though they represent your grand qualities."

Such sweet words spoken by the *eshq* (love) of his life caused emotion to overtake Lamar. His heart filled to the brim with adoration for Zuli, standing before him. She looked at him with a teasing smile.

"You're so well informed," whispered Lamar before gently touching the side of Zuli's face. "Please remember that, here and now, I love you more than ever – for who you are and what you represent. I don't believe I possess grand qualities, my golden sunflower. What I have is a meager, simple life. However, I do possess a true love for you, engraved on the four walls of my heart. This true love takes its essence from your splendor. Zuli, once we return to the Garden of Ali Mardan, no matter what happens, remember that I will always love you more than ever before."

At that moment, they realized the fairy-like hummingbirds began moving away from them.

"I think we should follow them, Lamar. I mean, I don't know how to get back to Sadaf. Do you have any clue which way to go?"

"I also don't know. Let's do it." At once, Lamar switched sides and walked to Zuli's left with his arm around her waist, holding her close.

After a long walk behind the line of brilliant birds with iridescent feathers, they came to an opening. They saw Sadaf, her massive white wings spread. Lamar and Zuli stopped in their tracks. They looked at one another, then back to Sadaf. She was surrounded by smaller doves and a parliament of owls. While the doves were primarily white, the owls were brown and orange, with touches of white here and there. They had strong, hooked beaks and powerful talons. Their eyes were sharp and wise in their large heads. The owls' faces were covered in clumps of white, stiff feathers sticking out. The same feathers surrounded their eyes, legs, and feet. To top it all off, they had enormous ears on the sides of their heads, and they were focused on the two visitors with grand intensity.

"Beautiful birds, aren't they?" Lamar asked, touching the tip of his own nose. "You don't think that my nose is as hooked as their beaks, do you Zuli?"

Zuli burst out laughing. This caught the attention of all the families of birds busy around Sadaf.

"Oh no, your nose is not as hooked, Lamar. Please stop. It's *their* beaks that aren't quite a match to your nose." Lamar hesitantly laughed, but continued to feel the tip of his nose until Zuli had to playfully slap his hand away from his face.

They were face-to-face, or rather, nose-to-beak,

with the owls. All the various birds gave Sadaf a complete checkup. They made sure she was in tip-top shape after being held in captivity for such a long time. Before long, the precise time to leave the fields of sunflowers and proceed home arrived.

They rose in the air, and flew in silence for a few minutes before Sadaf began to sing. The two enjoyed her angelic voice and listened to the lyrics: "I am Sadaf, known as the mother dove, expanding my wings to protect those who cannot fend for themselves. I fly high through the sky. I spread love and remain devoted. And that is why I am named Sadaf."

Lamar decided to pull out Zuli's love letter. He saw Zuli blush, but before she could object, he opened the folded letter and asked her if she would do him the honor of reading it to him. With a touch of bashfulness, she nervously took the letter from his hand, and leaned into his comfortable embrace. She began to read her confession of love to the man of her heart.

Zuli read with deliberation. "*Dearest Lamar* – seriously, are you sure you want me to read this to you?" she asked, looking timid.

"I certainly do, Zuli. And I shall read the letter I wrote to you too so that you understand the different depths and layers of each word. Each word took life, rose from my essence, was chosen by the pen of my heart, and printed on the paper I took from your notebook under the lemon trees in the Garden of Lily Ponds. Please continue."

Zuli nervously giggled. She cleared her throat as if speaking to a large audience. "*Dearest Lamar, long ago, I saw a painting of a fairyland...*"

By the time Zuli and Lamar finished reading their love letters aloud, they knew there was nowhere to go but deeper into loving one another, as was intended by fate. Despite having Sadaf in sight, and Zuli's lingering fear of heights, she took a deep breath and turned to face Lamar while still in his arms. He did not move. Then and there, Zuli released the social constraints taught to her as a young girl in a male-dominated society. She touched his handsome face, leaned in, and kissed the man who stole her heart like a bandit without a flicker of fright, openly in the daylight.

Pulling from each other's arms, Zuli was relieved to see Lamar was also overwhelmed by emotions. They wiped the tears of joy from one another's faces. They knew their tears were not only from the joy of finding love, but were also for the unknown bleak future that awaited them. So, to change the mood between them, Zuli ran her fingers over the words written in Lamar's handwriting.

"I love your handwriting," Zuli said. "It looks more like art than regular penmanship."

"Thank you, love. My father also had an immaculate handwriting. His handwriting did not resemble anyone else's – it looked as if it had been printed by a calligrapher. Ever since I was a kid, I admired his handwriting. In fact, I wanted to share this with you, and this is the perfect moment." From his pocket, Lamar pulled out a worn square of paper. "My father wrote this and gave it to me as a keepsake. This piece of paper is my most prized possession, evidence of my father's many talents, including his penmanship. May I read it to you?"

"Of course," Zuli replied.

"This is a poem by the great Hafiz."

آنان که خاک را به نظر کیمیا کنند

آیا بود که گوشه چشمی به ما کنند

Zuli took the delicate piece of paper from Lamar and marveled. "Thank you for sharing it with me. This is indeed such a profound verse. To me, it reads as, *those who turn dust to gold by a glance – could it be to have a corner glance at us.* If I may suggest, in order to preserve this artifact for a significantly long time, you should consider framing it once we return."

"That's a splendid idea, Zuli. I will do just that. Do you think we should call out to Sadaf to ask how far along we are? She's been quiet." Lamar queried, "Do you think she's fallen asleep? Let's just pray that she's wide awake considering that we're above the clouds. Oh, sorry, my love." He apologized and pulled Zuli closer to him when he saw her shudder at the thought of being so very high in the air on the back of a sleeping dove.

"Of course she's awake," reassured Zuli.

"Of course I'm awake, you two," Sadaf interjected.

"There's no need to panic. We were ahead of schedule, so I went the long way so you could enjoy a different view. It is coming up very soon. Now, if you two lovebirds can peel your eyes from one another, look out for beauty beyond your imagination."

Lamar and Zuli blushed at Sadaf's candid comments, but they did not stop clinging to one another.

In seconds, the green below changed to resemble the blue overhead. Lamar's eyes widened as he tried to comprehend what he saw, limitless beneath Sadaf's wings. It was the ocean. Zuli could not help but notice Lamar's expression of shock; he was taken by surprise. Just then, she understood that he had never before seen the ocean.

"That's called aquamarine," Zuli said, holding Lamar's hand and enjoying the look of disbelief plastered on his face.

Lamar took a deep breath and said, "Yet another gift of boundless beauty and pleasure from the powers beyond us." He looked out at the vastness of blue that not only covered them from above, but also spread out underneath them.

Sadaf said, "Lamar, I understand that you've never seen the ocean, so this is my gift as a thank you. You have journeyed such lengths with your travel companion, Zuli, to bring freedom to the wings that now proudly carry you. I'm going to fly lower and lower until I'm just above the water's surface."

Lamar thanked Sadaf over and over again, then turned to Zuli and said, "I've never seen such an outspread of blueness in one concentrated location. You know, even the beauty of the lily ponds pale in comparison." Lamar could not tell exactly what color the ocean was because the reflecting sun added hints of silvery green and fiery gold to the mix. At the same time, the grand sun was impressive and bathed him with warmth. The sky was painted with shades of coral and smudges of yellow, just like the sunflowers. He was witnessing heaven and it felt as though it was just a reach away.

As Sadaf got closer and closer to the surface of the water, it appeared to be a spotless mirror, with royal blue waves pulling one's sight to its swaying swellings. He was flooded with hope; a glimpse of a bright future flashed before his eyes, and a surging flame erupted in the center of his heart.

"Love, can you see the waves?" Zuli inquired.

"Yes, I see them. They're much more majestic than the currents I've seen in the rivers. Wow! Do you see the ocean floor and the fish of all sizes, Zuli?"

"I do see it all. It's truly *zaibaa* (beautiful). You know, Lamar, let's promise to one day travel the seas and swim the depths of the ocean with the aquatic life, as we did in the lily ponds."

"I promise, my love – so long as one of those aquatic animals is not related to the pufferfish from the ponds and doesn't show up to feast on us. I know when it sees my handsome face, it'll go for you first and save me for dessert."

Zuli laughingly retorted, "I guarantee you that, after taking one bite out of you, it'll lose its appetite for a lifetime."

Sadaf flew closer to the seawater that twinkled with tinted shades of pale turquoise, as if diamonds were scattered across the surface. As Lamar watched the rolling tides beneath them, he was struck by the introspective concept that *life is more like ocean waves; it all looks alike, but is never the same.* Zuli and Lamar laughed aloud as Sadaf went close enough to the water to splash them over and over again.

"If I could, I would land on the ocean, but I fear that it might get late, so off we go now. Hold on tight," Sadaf called out.

Chapter 7

The New Beginning

The mountain peaked. A few kites were in sight upon the canvas of high noon. It was all too familiar to Zuli and Lamar. Their journey had come to an end. On Friday, at the expected moment in time, they had returned to the magical domain of the Garden of Ali Mardan.

Zuli looked around; it had already been over five hours since Sadaf descended upon the garden where Adir awaited. So much had happened and so many important notions were discussed within those hours. The time was now early evening, just a tad past teatime. Zuli envisioned the palace staff busily putting away tea pots and china to begin the ritual of preparing for dinner. They were not a minute early or late in their arrival to the enchanted grounds. At least, that was what Lamar called the garden, seeing the mountains and kites against the vivid blue Kabul sky.

Adir received them with much enthusiasm and a warm, solid embrace. Yes, Lamar and Zuli were both asked for hugs. Of course, Lamar leapt to do so, but then caught himself mid-way and ushered Zuli to go first. Zuli smiled at his grandiose gestures when he put one hand behind his back, the other on his chest, and took a deep bow.

"Princess Zuli, you may go first, and I, your devoted

admirer, shall follow."

After Lamar hugged Adir, he braced himself to do as he and Zuli had discussed on the final leg of their flight. Lamar faced Adir and said, "Our wise friend and loyal protector, Adir, we bring good news and bad news. The good news is that we bring best wishes from your fond friends throughout the mystical gardens. The gracious Lilith, who is no longer with us but remains close to our hearts, sent you her never-ending blessings. The brilliant tulip, Almaas, in spirit, remains grateful and glowing. The prudent and formidable Kasib sends his heartfelt greetings. The score of fish families and Queen Shahbanu Sanam send their utmost thankfulness. The noble Mr. Matek sends his highest degree of *ahtaraam* (respect). Madam Tueti and all of the families of doves send their unwavering appreciation and cheers."

Lamar watched Adir's face brighten more and more at the mention of his enchanted friends. Lamar continued, "But above all, Zuli and I..."

Before he could finish, Lamar heard Sadaf flutter her wings and step forward. "My utmost apologies, dear Sadaf, I did not mean to leave you out! I wanted to save the best for last."

"Oh, no need for formalities; I have to head back anyway. I would first like to express my sincere and heartfelt appreciation to my grand friend, Adir. On behalf of Madam Tueti, my dove clan, and the wise owls, I simply thank you. We're beyond appreciative. We're free of all pain and suffering, and have gained much knowledge not only about self-protection, but also about protecting others. Furthermore, I would like to add my *tashakoraat* (thanks) to Princess Zuli and Lord Lamar for their kindness. Their connection comes from their enlightened souls and takes life from the seeds of love and humanity sown within them long ago. Lamar and Zuli, you have an ancient, *eshq derina* (eternal love). Thus, you were put on this earth at this very time to help others. Always listen to your inner voice. It shall never fail you, but rather will guide you to fulfill your goals. Remember these words, and I shall always carry you on my wings: go with the love of the Creator to reach your true potential. It is our sole purpose in this fleeting world to love all humanity."

With that, they watched Sadaf, the mother dove, sweep off the ground and fly in a big circle above them, saying, "We arrived at noon and it is now precisely 12:22. I must bid you all farewell. Just like the newfound friends you met along your journey, you, too, shall live in different gardens of colors and shapes, but know that you share one heart and that it beats to the same rhythm. As you grow older, the meanings of my lessons shall change with the wisdom that comes from the passage of time." Sadaf then flew east.

Reluctant, Lamar and Zuli faced Adir. The companions gave each other supportive looks and thought, *now, the bad news has to be told*. Lamar took a deep breath and, somewhat nervous, began to speak.

"As I said earlier, we also have bad news. Above all, Zuli and I remain indebted to you for granting us this inspiring and exhilarating opportunity to travel beyond our wildest imaginations through the mystifying gardens. We made friends and learned invaluable lessons about loyalty and how to help others in need."

Lamar took Zuli's hand as she stood motionless at his left, and, looking at her, hinted, "Isn't that so, Zuli?"

"Yes, it's true. We are in awe from what we experienced on our journey. But what we are trying to tell you is that we have come back empty-handed."

There, she had said it. It was out now. They watched Adir's face, their hearts beating at an alarming rate. Adir's tiny eyes narrowed ever so slowly. *They can't get any smaller*, Zuli thought to herself. Lamar squeezed her hand for support.

Zuli continued, "Please understand that we did everything in our power to retrieve the unseen fig blossom. Lamar climbed all the fig trees in The Garden of Roses. We searched through the leaves and branches of the fig trees that were, once again, green and free from the claws of the crows. Upon witnessing those magnificent trees regain their liveliness, we realized what the color green signifies and how it is invaluable, more so than the shiniest jewels. We now understand that green is precious, for it has the elements of life. Thus, each leaf on every tree dances in the heart of nature by the melodies of the wind. If Sadaf was still here, she could attest to our desperate search. As you know, Sadaf was on a time schedule to reach you no later than noon."

At this point, Adir widened his eyes. He stared at them both, back and forth, as their nervous energy reached its peak.

"I know this must be a great disappointment to you, Adir. It is as disappointing to Zuli and me. We sincerely apologize."

Adir's booming voice filled the air around them as he spoke, dust flying from his mouth. "Now, now, there is no need for apologies. Everyone but the two of you knew there was no such thing as the fig blossom."

Adir watched a wave of shock appear and disappear on their faces. He let out a thundering, yet somewhat comforting laugh, causing those magical pebbles to fall from his mouth at their feet. "You see, long ago, you were ordained to bring enlightenment and structure to society. Even before embarking upon your journey in search of the fig blossom, you helped in many different ways to eliminate ignorance, give rise to hope, and rebuild through teaching one individual at a time." He turned his attention to Lamar. "My young son, your grandfather knew that you left on this journey with a heart of gold, and have come back with the same golden heart now adorned with jewels. At every challenge, you did not think of yourself. You aided others to bring serenity to those in need. Know that you were both selfless givers. This brings us to the legendary tale of the fig blossom." Adir's voice echoed and his gaze never left the faces of his young friends.

Adir continued, "Now, here is the story of the unseen blossom.

As you two are well aware, you were chosen for this journey as the seekers of the fig blossom for two reasons: the first was to learn the teachings of selflessness in the course of your mystical voyage, which, in reality, served as a school of goodwill. The challenges were designed to enable you to see beyond your own needs and desires, and instead make decisions based on empathy for the betterment of others. Now, if you will, let us focus on the word "empathy." This happens to be my favorite word because it refers to having the ability to link the heart and mind to all creations in the world. If everyone reached into their conscience to commune with their innate sense of right and wrong, the world would turn by the wheels of harmony rather than by the forces of terror. For example, I'm sure you know about the good and bad in the nature of all crows. As we see in most creations, there are two sides – the bright and dark. In addition to their dark nature, crows also possess distinctive spirituality that symbolizes intelligence, power, and fearlessness. By the hands of time and experience, the crows in the Garden of Roses can undergo a positive transformation.

Empathy can be found far and wide throughout the world and, in possessing this quality, one can recognize the misfortune and pain of other living forms. Once the importance of this is understood, individuals can evolve, meaning that they can grow and advance to develop em-

pathetic qualities and abilities. Lamar and Zuli, you two are of the human family, connected regardless of color, creed, or beliefs. Therefore, it is vital that you can eventually teach people the importance of expanding serenity and tranquility from one corner of this equally shared space to another.

Your world is a gift with tiers of offerings and rewards; it is an invaluable treasure that is there for your discovery. You will realize that people value luxury more than they value the earth they stand upon and will take whatever means necessary to preserve their goods. It is essential to note that humans, in reality, are the heart of the earth, and the pulse for existence and immortality.

Now, the second reason for your journey brings me to you, Lamar. As a very young child, I am sure you recall observing a small fig tree with no blossoms on a street near your house in Kabul. Out of your relentless curiosity, your father brought you to the Garden of Ali Mardan, the home of the fig tree. Keep in mind, it was this curiosity that prompted you, as Zuli stated earlier, to climb practically all the fig trees in the Garden of Roses and search for the fig blossom, to no avail. Your favorite poet, Rumi, once said, "Maybe you are searching among the branches, for what only appears in the roots." This means that everyone and everything are intertwined, connected by the root of all creation.

The intention behind the creation of the first being was pure love. Know that the beauty of God was profoundly and equally exemplified in all of mankind. It is well known that the mystical fig blossom was first seen by the human eye. Since human beings were created to mirror their Creator's splendor, the blossom of the fig closed upon itself, yielding and submitting to His perfect creation. In essence, even the blossom became a selfless giver and offered itself as a heavenly gift in the form of a fruit – the fig. When the blossom closed upon itself, it remained unseen.

Lamar, the last words spoken by your grandfather were, "Blissfulness is to see love on the faces and in the hearts of fellow human beings in the garden of humanity." You will discover, through the different passages and stages of life, that humanity is based on serving one another with affection while continuing to seek and promote the best in others. We are forever knotted tightly as one family.

Yes, your grandfather possessed magical powers and was the keeper of the fig tree you have both admired since you were young. He knew that such a blossom no longer existed and would never grant harmony to your homeland, quite unlike how your wishes were instantly fulfilled by the magical branch he gave you. You were the chosen ones for the enchanted journey, which is why the key was left to you, Lamar. The ultimate goal was to achieve the spiritual depths that your grandfather possessed.

As you stand before me, I see two brilliant and charming young individuals destined to perform irreversible good deeds for mankind. I know that you are dedicated *to bringing unity and solidarity to the populace you admire. You also believe that leaders in society have a solemn obligation to lead by the virtue of grand example. Indeed, all facets of life require astute leaders. However, the lesson missing in the school of life is that all living organisms, especially human beings, are the byproduct of the foundations laid in earlier life. The people of a nation must learn that future leaders and role models are raised within the four walls of a home. This is the only way the early seeds of amity and morality will take root, strongly affixed to principles of righteousness and nobility. These codes of conduct could guide every person forward to achieve the ultimate wish of humanity – a promise for hope.*

Remember, as of this moment, the pages of your young lives are pure and clean. Others will follow your example and guidance. The sky of my soul is an endless expansion – it is clear of all clouds of doubt about your ability to soar. You must believe that the sun of life shall rise again to give new vigor and hope to where it is needed most. Yet, you will face battles and their lingering shadows. You shall deal with countless challenges and oppositions. It is imperative during these times that you push onward, keeping faith alive. In every new day there is a horizon; be sure to rise even when all else fails. Follow the teachings of wisdom you have learned from your mystical friends throughout the enchanted eastward and westbound journeys. A heart full of love and passion, in its inherent nature, shall lead you to wisdom. Of course, you remember retrieving the unique lotus flower that you gave to Queen Sanam in the Garden of Lily Ponds. Well, in Buddhism, they believe that, "to blossom in the sun, the lotus flower must first grow through muck and mud, a phenomenon that may serve as a moving metaphor for our own spiritual paths."

The true blossom of love is already within you. The responsibility lies with each person to open their heart and see the magic of the blossomless fig, just as clearly as you see shades of color in the morning dawn. Never forget that service in the way of humanity is one of the most sacred human bonds. The mere fact of being chosen to serve is the highest of callings.

Your young hearts are filled with the zest of life, which will fuel you with, as Tueti would say, joie de vivre (joy of life). Such dynamic sparks will compel you to diligence and unity. Humans utilize such traits to direct or redirect those whose paths have not been illuminated by their innate goodness.

Go now! Turn on the light for one and for all to see, from the backstreets and high mountains of your motherland to the great beyond. As ambassadors of peace, you shall remain in the garden of humanity for the sake of saving the links of connection within the circle of your human family.

While Zuli listened to Adir, she realized that the brutality of war must not be an option when trying to reach global concord. Her attention shifted to Lamar as he thanked Adir for the wise teachings.

Lamar was mindful of the hardships awaiting him and addressed Adir, "I know that our nation has been under siege. Flowers must grow on all the surfaces of our motherland. Within the folds of our land are the lost lives of the young, old, and innocent.

"If only millions of hands would join together to arise from the dust of misery and bloodshed! This can only be achieved with the linkage of an interconnected chain of unity, unbreakable in the hands of the oppressor, the enemy of mankind. Zuli and I understand that Earth's supreme beauty can only be found within the human race. People must be valued, otherwise pandemonium will ensue."

Lamar looked at Zuli, and asked, "Are you okay, my love?"

Zuli smiled at him reassuringly, although her thoughts lingered on her fear. What would become of them once they left the enchanted garden, where they freely expressed their love? They would never have such freedom in the streets or gardens of Kabul. They could not hold hands in public. Oh, how she loved Lamar, who had suffered the burdens of life in such a short span. He was educated and talented, but worked at a shoe repair shop. Granted, he was too proud and may not accept her offer, but she would try to help him get a job that he qualified for and deserved. She could not see herself being apart from him for even a blink of an eye.

How would she ever tell her mother about Lamar? Her mother had already selected a handful of young men for Zuli to consider as her future life partner. Already, Zuli felt the aching pain of separation. She felt waves of tears crawling steadily from the shores of her heart, ready to drown her. She had wept when Lamar recounted his life story early on their journey. He had said something about her tears being purer than all the pearls in the depths of the ocean. Well, in that moment, her tears were painful and pure. She did not want Adir or Lamar to see her cry, so she took a deep breath and told herself to never lose sight of hope.

Zuli knew that she and Lamar would have colossal challenges ahead. After all, they were chosen to bring the message of love to a war-ravaged nation. They now realized that, in order to build a more benevolent institution, the pillars of such an establishment must be made from a unified nation marching peacefully in one direction. Their purpose was to rebuild, replant, and rejuvenate the roots sown by men and women of the past. It was their own ancestors who rested in the earth, now saturated with the blood of innocents. As the fig blossom is both a flower and fruit in one, the people of a nation must be of one *qualb* (heart) and from one source of love.

Adir was thoughtful and allowed them to spend a few private moments alone.

"I suppose Adir knows that we will not have this time together once we cross over," Lamar expressed. He held Zuli's hands and kissed them, one at a time, before wrapping her in his warm embrace.

Zuli looked at the towering young man who held her in his arms. She stood on her tiptoes and kissed and kissed Lamar until they heard Adir's voice. He cleared his throat, causing pebbles to fall and dust to billow around them.

"This journey began in the Garden of Ali Mardan, and it must end exactly where it began. The lessons will stay with you; while the memories of your mystical journey shall fade, the love in your hearts will find ways to flourish. The fair hands of fate will guide your steps across familiar paths. Give time the benefit of the doubt to come back around as it was originally intended. Lastly, remember that, on the very last word of the third enchantment, you shall find yourselves back in the exact time and place you were before going through the fig tree." Adir concluded with, "I, the steadfast and sturdy old rock, shall stay the keeper of the enchanted gardens."

Zuli and Lamar held the silver-tipped magical branch one final time. They pointed it towards Adir, who bid them a resounding farewell.

The third enchantment was: *The unseen blossom is the love within your heart. Give it with no haste. Hold tight and hope with all your might. It will lead you to new heights.*

Zuli opened her eyes with a start. For a split second, she could not remember where she was. Then she felt the fig tree against her back; she must have dozed off.

Oh my, what time is it? She jumped to her feet, clutching her notebook. Zuli ran towards the palace.

She had dreamt a most unusual dream, and her mind was still racing with all the sounds and faces she encountered.

Caught up in her thoughts, Zuli picked up speed, turned the corner, and veered right as she had done a thousand times before. Unlike every other time, this time, Zuli ran head-first into a young man. She threw him entirely off his feet; he landed on the dusty road against a mud wall.

Lamar picked himself up and looked at the beautiful face staring at him as if she saw a ghost. Her eyes left his face and rested on his hands. He looked down and saw that he held a quite familiar object. It was a sturdy tree branch with a silver tip. A glimpse of recognition flickered between their intimate gazes before Zuli turned fast on her heels and headed towards the palace. She looked back and shouted at the stunned young man still rooted to the same spot.

"My name is Zuli and I am sorry for tripping you! I do hope you are not hurt too badly." Again, in a split second, traces of intimacy flashed with ease like a summer breeze between them. "I live just around the corner. Since my mother is very strict, I cannot be late for supper at eight. I shall return tomorrow to check on you. Meet me under the fig tree in the Garden of Ali Mardan. Forget me not."

THE END

Wednesday September 7, 2016

11:01 a.m.

"Dew drops from an early dawn narcissus
as if tear drops from a melancholy eye,
O beauty, I asked, what makes you cry
life is too short for me, it answered
My beauty blooms and withers in a moment
as if smile comes and forever fades away."
~ Nazo Tokhi

RESOURCES

Learn more about the book, authors, poets, sites and characters:

Amazon:	The Unseen Blossom by Zlaikha Y. Samad and L'mere Younossi
Facebook:	TheUnseenBlossomBook
Twitter:	@UnseenBlossom
Instagram:	theunseenblossom

The authors invite the readers to share their comments and feedback by writing to TheUnseenBlossom@yahoo.com

"If you doubt this phenomenon, such an extraordinary wonder, then ask yourself: have you ever seen a fig tree bloom?"

http://www.plantanswers.com/garden_column/aug04/1.htm

The Garden of Ali Mardan

https://en.wikipedia.org/wiki/Ali_Mardan_Khan

Ali Mardan Khan was a Kurdish military leader serving under the Safavid governor of Qandahar. On being dismissed from office, he sought assistance from the governor of Kabul and commander of Ghazni. In 1638, he surrendered Qandahar to the Mughals, and took refuge in Delhi. He later received the title of Amir al-Umara (Lord of Lords) leading an army of 7,000 troops.

He was the son of Ganj Ali Khan. He died in April 1657 in Lahore – his tomb is located on Mughalpura Road in Lahore, Pakistan. A garden was named after him in Kabul, Afghanistan, and a garden was named after him still survives in Srinagar Kashmir.

Darul Aman Palace

https://en.wikipedia.org/wiki/Darul_Aman_Palace

Darul Aman Palace ("abode of peace") is a European-style palace located about sixteen kilometers (ten miles) outside of the center of Kabul, Afghanistan.

Rabia Balkhi - Afghan poet

https://en.wikipedia.org/wiki/Rabia_Balkhi

Rābi'a bint Ka'b al-Quzdārī (Persian: رابعہ بنت کعب), popularly known as Rābi'a Balkhī (رابعہ بلخی) and Zayn al-'Arab[1] (زین العرب), is a semi-legendary[2] figure of Persian literature and was possibly the first woman poet in the history of New Persian poetry. References to her can be found in the poetry of Rū-dakī and ʿAttār. Her biography has been primarily recorded by Zāhir ud-Dīn 'Awfī and renarrated by Nūr ad-Dīn Djāmī. The exact dates of her birth and death are unknown, but it is reported that she was a native of Balkh in Khorāsān (Afghanistan).

Ludwig von Beethoven

https://en.wikipedia.org/wiki/Ludwig_van_Beethoven

Ludwig von Beethoven was a German composer. A crucial figure in the transition between the Classical and Romantic eras in Western art music, he remains one of the most famous and influential of all composers.

Rangwali Holi

https://en.wikipedia.org/wiki/Holi

Holi is a Hindu spring festival in India and Nepal, also known as the festival of colors or the festival of sharing love.

Saint Basil

https://en.wikipedia.org/wiki/Basil_of_Caesarea

Basil of Caesarea, also called Saint Basil the Great, was the Greek bishop of Caesarea Mazaca in Cappadocia, Asia Minor (modern-day Turkey).

Rumi

https://en.wikipedia.org/wiki/Rumi

Jalāl ad-Dīn Muhammad Rūmī, also known as Jalāl ad-Dīn Muhammad Balkhī, Mawlānā/Mevlânâ ("our master"), Mevlevî/Mawlawī ("my master"), and more popularly simply as Rumi, was a 13th-century Persian poet, jurist, Islamic scholar, theologian, and Sufi mystic. Born: September 30, 1207, Balkh, Afghanistan, Died: December 17, 1273, Konya, Turkey

Paghman

https://en.wikipedia.org/wiki/Paghman

Paghman is a town in the hills near Afghanistan's capital of Kabul. The Paghman District is situated in the western part of Kabul Province. The Paghman Gardens is a major attraction in Paghman, and is why the city is sometimes known as the capital garden of Afghanistan.

Oscar-Claude Monet

https://en.wikipedia.org/wiki/Claude_Monet Oscar-Claude Monet

French; (14 November 1840 – 5 December 1926) was a founder of French Impressionist painting...Monet's ambition of documenting the French countryside led him to adopt a method of painting the same scene many times in order to capture the changing of light and the passing of the seasons. From 1883 Monet lived in Giverny, where he purchased a house and property, and began a vast landscaping project which included lily ponds that would become the subjects of his best-known works. In 1899 he began painting the water lilies, first in vertical views with a Japanese bridge as a central feature, and later in the series of large-scale paintings that was to occupy him continuously for the next 20 years of his life.

Baidel

https://en.wikipedia.org/wiki/Abdul-Q%C4%81dir_B%C4%ABdel Mawlānā Abul-Ma'ānī Mīrzā Abdul-Qādir Bēdil

(or Bīdel) also known as Bīdel Dehlavī (1642 – 1720), was a famous representative of Persian poetry and Sufism in India. He is considered the most difficult and challenging poet of Safavid-Mughal poetry.

تبسم از لبت چون موج در گوهر کند بازی

نسیم از طرہات چون فتنه در محشر کند بازی

Translation by L'mere Younossi:

"The smile on your lips plays like a wave on pearls...the breeze in your hair fooling around as a devil in mayhem."

Tabla

https://en.wikipedia.org/wiki/Tabla

The tabla is a membranophone percussion instrument (similar to bongos) which is often used in Hindustani classical music and in the traditional music of Afghanistan, India, Pakistan, Nepal, Bangladesh, and Sri Lanka. The instrument consists of a pair of hand drums of contrasting sizes and timbres.

روز ها گر رفت گو رو باک نیست
تو بمان ای آنکه چون تو پاک نیست

Translation by L'mere Younossi:

"Days that are gone, say go, it matters not – You stay, none are purer than you." – Rumi

آنان که خاک را به نظر کیمیا کنند
آیا بود که گوشه چشمی به ما کنند

Translation by L'mere Younossi:

"Those who turn dust to gold by a glance – could it be to have a corner glance at us." – Hafiz

Nazo Tokhi – Afghan poet and warrior

https://en.wikipedia.org/wiki/Nazo_Tokhi

Nāzo Tokhī, commonly known as Nāzo Anā ("Nazo the grandmother"), was a Pashtun female poet and a literary figure of the Pashto language. Mother of the famous early-18th century Afghan King Mirwais Hotak, she grew up in an influential family in the Kandahar region. Nazo Tokhi is remembered as a brave woman warrior in the history of Afghanistan, who eventually became the legendary "Mother of Afghan Nation."

Thanks to Janice Bell, Facebook member, for the quote in Chapter 5:

"Yes, be a waterfall; erode and wash away the sharp, nasty edges of corruption, all while remaining true to the beauty of nature."

"To blossom in the sun, the lotus flower must first grow through muck and mud, a phenomenon that may serve as a moving metaphor for our own spiritual paths."

https://www.buddhagroove.com/reversible-lotus-pendant-necklace-inspirational-necklace/

ABOUT THE AUTHORS

ZLAIKHA Y. SAMAD

(Zlaikha Samad Sadozai)

Over the years, I was encouraged to write a book. I attempted countless times, but to no avail. The day I met my friend, I sensed an internal shift within me. A certain awareness or intuition, if you will, gave rise to specific scenes, ideas, and words. Soon after my unexpected connection with L'mere, he posed a question to me: "Have you ever seen a fig tree bloom?" He proceeded to tell me about the idea of the blossomless fig tree and his wish to write a book surrounding it. Intuitively, I knew that I was meant to co-write this book with him, but it seemed impossible because I was not an author. Unbeknownst to me, there was a novel waiting to be poured out of me onto blank pages. Hence, *The Unseen Blossom* was born between us.

I am an Afghan-American born in Kabul, Afghanistan, and I came to the USA as a political refugee in 1981. I am lucky to be from an intellectual family of diplomats, writers, professors, physicians, travel enthusiasts, and peacemakers.

I am a new author. Before this, I had only ever written freeform poems. It is somewhat difficult to explain, but the soul connection between us is the driving force behind the creation of our book.

Our story can be passed down to awaken and strengthen one's sense of humanity. This fairytale novel illustrates our world's magnificence weaved within a love story of two young souls.

Throughout this experience, I am most proud to be the mother of my wonderful daughter and brilliant junior editor, Madee. She is my heart.

Last but not least, I wholeheartedly thank my husband, Wais, for his support. I remain grateful.

L'MERE YOUNOSSI

I am an Afghan-American who came to the USA in 1965 and, to my chagrin, never again returned to the motherland. I earned my master's degree in international business from Pace University, located in New York City. I am also a self-taught man with an insatiable thirst for knowledge. Foremost, I am a fervent student with a blazing flame of desire for uncovering life, music, art, literature, philosophy, and the humanities. I have dedicated ample time to reading and writing poems in different languages, which I then post on Facebook for the pure enjoyment of my family and friends.

I am elated to tell you about a dream I once had; I was in the midst of a rainstorm. Complete darkness enveloped me within an uproarious downpour. Unexpectedly, I looked up to see an onrushing object approaching at an alarming speed. I knew that I was supposed to catch it, so I did just that. As soon as I caught the unknown object, I awoke, sitting upright with my hands in the air. Believe me: it was a book that fell from the stormy skies.

The seed of this book was instilled within me at a young age. I was bewildered by the reality of a tree that had no blossom yet still produced fruit, and it was here that this phenomenon took root within my mind.

However, this book was born when, once again, in another dream, I saw myself sharing the story of the blossomless fig tree with Zlaikha, the one with whom it was meant to be written.

A Compelling and Thrilling Read

The Unseen Path

*Sequel to
The Unseen Blossom*

"The Unseen Path *is full of stunning imagery and poetic language. It is a story of love and hope that blends age-old wisdom with modern themes. Readers will go on a journey through its pages..."*

Deborah Ellis, an award-winning author of the international bestseller The Breadwinner Trilogy.

The Unseen Path is a work of fiction in the adventure, interpersonal drama, and romance subgenres, and was penned by author duo Zlaikha Y. Samad and L'mere Younossi. The sequel to The Unseen Blossom, *we have previously seen our central protagonists Zuli and Lamar meet within a fantastical fantasy world where they searched for the mystical blossom that would bring healing to the grief of their nation. But back in the real world, Afghanistan is in deeper trouble than ever, and the new regime threatens to tear Zuli and Lamar apart forever. What follows is a poetically penned adventure tale that seeks to reunite hope and love even in the darkest circumstances.*

Adult and young adult readers alike have much to gain from the beautiful reading experience that author duo Zlaikha Y. Samad and L'mere Younossi have created. In this combination between reality and fantasy, there are many comparisons we can draw with our own lives and the oppressions and struggles which keep people apart and nations at war. Then, woven delicately into these poignant messages, we find the beautiful bond between the young protagonists Zuli and Lamar. One aspect I found particularly beautiful was the dialogue, which is laced with hope for the young people's futures but also discusses the harsh realities of life in a way that readers from all walks of life can understand. Overall, I would highly recommend The Unseen Path *as a fantastic adventure novel with many hidden depths for its readers to explore.*

Reviewed By K.C. Finn for Readers' Favorite

The Unseen
Path

Zuli and Lamar, after their surreal journey through fantastical gardens where they searched for the unseen blossom, find themselves in peril amid a brutal invasion that threatens their freedom and love. They are torn apart by the malicious hands of the oppressors and are trapped by unspeakable losses. Their beloved motherland of Afghanistan is no more, and the royals have been dethroned. Encircled by unforgettable faces, some new and some old, the fleeting pretense of normalcy is shattered. Are Zuli and Lamar able to reunite and return on their sacred path to love?

CPSIA information can be obtained
at www.ICGtesting.com
Printed in the USA
BVHW041459160221
R11873400001B/R118734PG599227BVX00010B/8